S uzi turned in her seat so she could look out the rear window. "I think someone is out there."

"Maybe someone looking for a cheap thrill," Joseph said. "Maybe one of those geeks has a crush on you or something."

"I don't know," Suzi said. "It sounded like a cough. Or a growl."

Somewhere outside a twig snapped.

Suzi twisted in her seat to look out a side window, and a scream issued from her lips. Joseph jerked around, ready to face whatever she saw. He almost fainted with relief when he realized nothing was there.

"You're just nervous," he said as the fear slowly diminished. "Relax. Nobody will catch us here."

He put his arm around her again, and reaching forward with his free hand he tilted her chin up slightly so he could kiss her.

She didn't pull away this time and the kiss lasted for several seconds.

It ended only when the fur-covered arm shot through the glass on the passenger side, sending glass shards spraying inward. Suzi screamed again, louder and louder.

The clawed hand was reaching for Joseph's throat.

DEADLY DELIVERY

SIDNEY WILLIAMS
WRITING AS MICHAEL AUGUST

For Sid, without whom this novel would not have been possible.

This all happened a long time ago, before we had e-mail and the Internet, X-Box and online gaming. We had to use our imagination to entertain ourselves. It got a little scary...

Chapter One

Monster Maker

"MAKE YOUR OWN MONSTER AND COMPETE IN MONSTROUS EXCITEMENT IN THE TERROR CLUB, A THRILLING NEW HORROR GAME YOU CAN PLAY BY MAIL."

The ad seemed to jump off the page of Derek Cliver's new copy of *Scare* magazine, and even though it was a little like kid stuff, the summer was dragging slowly enough to make any diversion seem promising. Tomorrow he'd be starting a summer acting workshop, but he had to survive the hours in between.

He'd had the subscription to *Scare* since he'd been twelve, and originally it had seemed exciting. He'd wanted to be a film director at the time, and *Scare* had helped him keep up with the horror-movie industry. Now it seemed a little behind him, but he still thumbed it even though he had just turned seventeen and was almost ready for his junior year in high school. He'd changed his mind about directing low-budget horror movies. After doing a play last semester he was becoming more serious about acting, and he didn't want to limit himself to playing dead teenagers.

On this endless summer afternoon, the magazine was to be the only thing to keep him from going completely bonkers, however. He was glad his subscription hadn't run out.

Sitting up on the bed where he'd been reclining against the pillows, he read further, his eyes darting down to the smaller print in the advertisement:

1

How to Play

Create the scariest monster you can imagine.

Write us a letter about your creature. Tell us what he looks like. Tell us about his powers.

Send the monster to Scare to the address listed below, and if we get scared we'll assign an artist to sketch the being for a "Monster Gallery" spread in a future issue.

You'll also be eligible to play in the new Scare competition with other monster makers. Enclose a self-addressed stamped envelope for details if you send by mail.

Brushing back a lock of his sandy hair, Derek slid immediately off the bed and hurried across the room to the old desk in the corner. A rolltop that had belonged to a distant uncle, it had become his storage space for pencils and other materials from the past school year. Maybe the game would keep him busy for a while, and creating a monster wasn't that removed from creating a character in a play. It might be a good exercise in imagination.

From one of the lower drawers, he picked out a notebook, the formerly bright yellow cover now cracked and marred by stickman drawings created during two semesters of dull lectures. The front pages were filled with notes and history assignments, but in the back there were still some blank sheets.

With a Papermate also leftover over from school, he wrote his return address as a heading and began to describe a beast as dire and dreadful as he could imagine. Memories of movie monsters and old H.P. Lovecraft stories fueled his thoughts as the pen scribbled out details—hideous features, horrible rasping breath and hulking size. It wasn't a werewolf, though he imagined it covered with fur. It wasn't a vampire, but he decided it could drink blood. It wasn't a zombie, yet he imagined it lumbering through the shadows, stalking, peering through the darkness with red glowing eyes capable of night vision.

Tiny bumps of gooseflesh began to form on his arms as he continued, making him chuckle at his own shudders as he jotted a few notes about the creature's claws and fangs. The feet would be like a second set of hands, the yellowed, jagged nails sharp as razors. He could picture it stalking the night, lurking through the neighborhoods.

The fur was thick and gray over the slightly stooped shoulder, partially because of the heavy musculature of the creature's chest and back. It had the basic form of a man, after all, a very massive and powerful man. The shape of the head would be a little more bestial, however, with ridges along the skull, not quite horns, but strong and pronounced though overgrown with wild tufts of hair. The eyes were not human at all. The pupils were slits, like a cat's, the lids thick hoods with thin tufts of hair shooting off them.

Satisfied with the horrific nature of the physical description, he decided to add an additional touch, the kind of depth he'd learned about in acting class, the extra layer that made a character seem real. He threw in a few lines about the creature's intelligence. It was not just some hulking brute, lurking through the night to commit mindless carnage against whatever unfortunate crossed its path. No, it was more formidable. It was an intelligent beast, a cunning haunt that could do more than lumber along. It was capable of trickery and unpredictable moves.

Derek had watched horror movies on late-night television, especially on nights his mom had dates and was not home to tell him he didn't need to be watching that sort of thing into the wee hours. Most of the flicks were pretty bad, but now and then he tuned in some good ones, and he found the ones that came closest to scaring him were those with monsters that managed to be more than killing machines.

Monsters that were clever, monsters that might outsmart you even if you were displaying more intelligence than the average teenager in a horror movie, were what made him shiver the most. One or two of those had done more than raise shivers.

They'd prompted him to turn the ceiling lights on and wait for the sound of tires pulling into the driveway even though he felt silly and childish. That was the curse of a fertile imagination, but he was getting too old to jump at creaks in the night.

At least it allowed him to create a great creature. Someone with just a little common sense might escape the average hairy ape, but a hairy ape with a genius IQ was another proposition.

He pointed that out in his final sentence, a closing statement which should win him a few contest points, he decided. Then he reread the entire piece. It filled a page and a half in the notebook. He'd managed to keep his handwriting neat throughout, but he considered rewriting, then decided against it.

This was a lark, not something as serious as an English paper, nor was it important enough to require meticulous effort. Ripping the pages out of the notebook, he took some scissors from a drawer and clipped off the jagged edges left by the spirals.

He had to go into his mom's room and rifle her desk for a stamp and envelope, but he decided she wouldn't miss just one of each. Her attention was more focused on Neil these days.

She'd met him at the supermarket and they spent almost all of their free time together. They were always going to movies or out to dinner, leaving Derek to fend for himself.

Sometimes Derek worried his mom was too smitten with Neil. The guy was almost too handsome and too smooth. He was like a grown-up jock. He obviously wanted to get married, but Derek didn't want a new father. He didn't really think his mom needed a new husband either. They'd done just fine before Neil had slipped into their lives.

He had a good job and was nice enough, but Derek didn't like the efforts Neil made to be a pal. He'd adjusted to living without his father. He didn't need a big brother. He and his mom had been happy before, but now she sometimes seemed like a schoolgirl. She didn't need to be dating. She needed to be a mom.

Derek knew he wasn't supposed to be upset about her having dates. That was childish, but he couldn't exactly help feeling a little neglected sometimes. Especially when there was nothing but television to pass the hours. His best friend, Logan, was away for the summer, and another really good friend, Peter Stamford, had moved away last year, so he didn't exactly have a crowd to hang around with in the vicinity.

At least acting class would give him something to do, he thought as he headed out the front door and climbed into the battered old used Mustang he drove. He'd signed up for the workshop to decide if he had some acting skills. The play had given him a taste of theater, but he still wasn't sure he was cut out for the work. People liked to rib him about being an "*ac-tor*" acting, and he wasn't fond of being teased.

Sometimes he wished he was a few pounds heavier and inclined toward football. Football players got the girls. Almost-skinny actors only turned heads if they managed to become movie stars.

But, he told himself, even Tom Cruise had to start somewhere. The sun was high and bright, and even though the air was hot, the day seemed fresh and newly exciting. Getting the creative juices flowing with a monster had lifted his funk a little.

He might be a long time hearing from the good folks at Scare, but at least they'd allowed him to pick up his spirits a little. If he had enough imagination to be a monster maker, maybe he could be a good actor, too.

Coaxing the old car's engine to life, he backed out of the driveway, ignoring the shudders and complaints. If he made a decent actor, he'd be able to afford a new car, someday.

Maybe he'd go into film and make some money, he thought. Maybe he'd make some serious films and then do a scary movie for the fun of it. Maybe he'd even use his monster. It could be wishful thinking, but he could give it a shot.

As his car coasted along the street that ran in front of the neat brick ranch-style houses of his neighborhood, he let his imagination conjure a monster movie set right here in Pembrook. He could picture his monster stalking this neighborhood, ducking behind the oak trees in some yards or crouching behind fences in others.. After all, there were plenty of places for a monster to hide.

Chapter Two

The New Girl

The acting workshop was scheduled in the Pembrook High gymnasium. While it was used mostly for basketball, the building had a large neglected stage. In recent years it had been used more for assemblies than plays, and the stage floor was scuffed and dingy while the old burgundy draperies were faded and smelled of dust.

Tables and metal chairs had been set up on the stage to accommodate the crowd of kids who showed up for the opening session. Derek wandered in through a side door as students began to cluster, their voices echoing through the cavernous gym. He was hoping to find some friends in the group, but he realized many of the faces were unfamiliar, or they were only people he knew in passing. Some were freshmen who wouldn't become full-time students at Pembrook until the fall. They were probably trying to get an early orientation so they'd be prepared to find their way around and know places to hide from senior hazing.

Other kids, he realized, were on hand because they wanted to get away from their parents. While their folks might not grant them liberty to go water skiing or engage in other summer activities, they would grant permission to go to school.

That was a little disheartening, because Derek had been hoping for a fun session. If there were a bunch of kids around who thought acting was geeky the whole summer was shot. He was not up to a competition among the in crowd.

He could tell that was how things would shape up when he saw Amber Sawyer and Craig Montgomery standing at the edge of the stage along with a brood of other kids from their social clique.

Amber and Craig were practically the king and queen of Pembrook High's aristocracy, and their subjects consisted of some of the worst snobs Derek had ever encountered. They tended to look down on any kid who didn't fit into their circle or who didn't wear clothes by the same designers they did.

Craig was the football-team captain, and he looked almost too perfect with a square jawed face and hair he kept trimmed and moussed into place. Today he was wearing an expensive pullover shirt and designer shorts that would have torpedoed Derek's allowance for months.

Amber was well suited for Craig. She had Caribbean blue eyes and wore her shiny blond hair trimmed in a neat shoulder-length style that framed a smooth heart-shaped face. She was beautiful, but Derek always found her looks severe. Her expression was one of perpetual dissatisfaction. Like Craig she was dressed this morning in designer clothes, a short white skirt and a blue blouse with her initials stenciled into the fabric.

The friends around them were equally well dressed and were exchanging expressions of disapproval as they viewed the other kids who entered. Derek watched them for a moment as they wrinkled their noses and rolled their eyes.

The snobs he recognized one and all. There was Joseph Stanley, a dark-haired version of Craig except that he was taller. He played on the basketball team. With Joseph was his girlfriend, Suzi Crandle. She'd been voted as one of the most beautiful girls on campus, a fact that was not arguable. She was a redhead with emerald eyes and a perfect figure, but her personality did not match her looks. She was always quick to spout her contempt for those she considered inferior.

Also standing in the group were Jude Sheffield, who was tall and thin with curly hair and freckles. He looked like a geek, but he had the most expensive clothes of any of them, and he drove a fiery red sports car that everybody envied. Everyone suspected the car was how he kept his girlfriend, Denise Hubbard, a brunette who headed the pep squad and was destined for the cover of a Sports Illustrated swimsuit edition someday. Derek suspected the jewelry Jude bought her didn't hurt either.

With this crowd, there was no way the workshop would be any fun. Derek knew he could give the performance of his lifetime and they'd only snicker or yawn and pat their open mouths, and he didn't need that kind of aggravation.

He could do better staying home and playing his Terror Club game. He was about to turn and make his way back to the door when someone else caught his eye.

She was about his age, but she could've passed for nineteen easy. She was beautiful, with dark hair that tumbled down her back in a mass of curls, and her form was slender at the waist yet full in the right places. She was wearing a blue tee shirt and white shorts, and he couldn't help but notice her long legs, tanned by the summer sun.

She looked like a candidate for the in crowd, but when she turned around, he got a look at her face. She lacked the snobbish expression. She had soft features, rounded cheeks, and brown eyes—big brown eyes. As the corners of her mouth turned up into a sweet smile, he realized his gaze must be locked on her.

He almost jerked his neck out of its socket as he turned his head toward the tables where some kids were already beginning to get seated. Only after a second did he let his head turn again, just slightly, so that he was looking at her once more. He managed a half smile in spite of his sudden feeling of stupidity.

"Hi," she said, as she took a couple of steps forward.

His reply was almost a croak, a hoarse sound from the back of his throat. This wasn't the kind of girl that noticed him. He felt dim-witted as she continued to smile, and he knew some color had crept into his cheeks. Her giggle confirmed it.

A tingling sting of embarrassment crept up through his legs as he tried to think of something to say, something that could redeem the situation. After all, he was looking at the best alternative to the summer doldrums he could imagine.

He'd only had a couple of girlfriends, never a steady really. He'd gone on bowling trips with groups and taken girls to sporting events or dances, but those things hadn't amounted to much. He was shy for the most part, uncertain of himself around girls. There weren't really that many girls around that he could talk to, certainly none as appealing as the one in front of him.

Possibilities of movie matinees and walks at dusk hit him. She must be new around here, which meant she was less likely to have a boyfriend. Something could happen, right here, right now—if he could just manage to form syllables, or at least to smile. He felt one corner of his mouth twitch, not quite a smile but not totally a smirk. At least ideas of making for the door had faded.

"So, you signing up for the workshop?" he asked. Stupid question. He didn't even have to consider what he'd said to realize that. Of course she was. Why else would she be here. What was he, a guidance counselor?

She giggled again. It wasn't a silly giggle, more an acknowledgment that he'd spoken. Maybe she didn't think he was a total idiot. "I just thought it would be something to pass the time," she said. "There's not a whole lot to do around here, is there?"

"No," he agreed. That was the easiest question he'd have all day. "It kind of drags in the summer. Everybody goes on vacation and everything."

He glanced back at the crowd for a second, then back at her. "Are you new in town?"

She nodded, and the movement made her curls bounce. "My dad just transferred," she said. "He's an accountant for the Stillwell Corporation."

"Yeah, they make household products."

"Um-hum. For the whole region."

"You like it okay? I mean Pembrook? Aside from the boredom."

"Well, I don't have many friends yet," she said.

Something inside him almost seemed to explode. He wanted to start singing like one of the guys in the old movies his mom liked.

No boyfriend!

"Well, you know, maybe I could show you around." He swallowed. He'd never really asked anyone out so casually. It wasn't as hard as he'd thought it might be, but things didn't seem quite real either.

"There's not much to see, is there?"

"Not much," he agreed. "There's a theater, and a mall."

"Teenagers can't survive without those, can they?"

"Not at all. There's a library, too."

"Sounds like quite a few sights. I think I'd like that, seeing the sights."

"Great. We'll make plans after class." He started to walk with her toward a table but then touched her arm. "Hey, I don't know your name," he said.

She laughed again, and smiled deeply enough to display dimples. "It's Paige," she said. "Paige Laningham."

He felt like he was about to burst as euphoria expanded. Let the snobs hit him with their attitudes. He could handle that if this workshop gave him a chance to be around Paige.

He was following her bouncy step toward a table near the edge of the stage when they heard the commotion. One of the metal chairs overturned, and the clatter of the metal striking the stage floor silenced all of the chatter, leaving only the echo of the noise off the far wall of the gym.

All eyes were turned toward one end of the stage near some rear curtains. Craig was standing there, his hands clutching the black tee-shirt collar of a kid almost a foot shorter than him. The kid was on his tiptoes, trying to pull away from the larger boy without success. His Reeboks couldn't get any traction.

Derek wondered what the kid had done to make Craig mad. He'd probably only looked at him wrong. It didn't take much to anger Craig, and the kid looked like a natural enemy.

He was thin and geeky with wire-rimmed glasses and longish black hair, and he was wearing baggy slacks and his tee shirt had a comic-book character on it.

"What's he doing to him?" Paige asked.

"That's Craig Montgomery," he said. "He's probably bored with being here and decided to ruin somebody else's day. He's a real jerk."

"Yeah, I made his acquaintance," Paige whispered.

Derek was about to ask how when Craig's voice thundered through the room. "Were you looking at my girlfriend?"

"Real mature guy," Derek said. He looked around, wondering where the teacher was. If she didn't show up, he was going to try and do something to keep the kid from getting his head busted and to keep from looking like a wimp in front of Paige. He didn't cherish the idea.

"I'm sorry," the little guy said, closing his hands around Craig's thick wrists and trying to pry himself free.

"That's not good enough," Craig said, lifting him a little higher.

Derek sighed. He might wind up getting hurt himself, but he had to do something. He was almost relieved as he stepped forward and saw that Alex Jackson had just stepped through a side door.

Alex, an African American guy with short-cropped hair and gold-rimmed glasses, was his friend, and he was also on the football team, though he didn't get to play as much as Craig. He wasn't quite as heavy as he needed to be to play on the line, but he was muscular.

"What's going on?" he asked.

"Craig's trying to pummel some new kid."

Alex's eyes rolled upward. "Doesn't he ever get tired?"

They walked together over to the spot where the torment was occurring. The kid was still trying to pull away, and Craig was laughing at him.

"That's enough," Alex said.

Craig looked up, his brow wrinkled with annoyance. He didn't like being disturbed.

"Who says, Jackson?" he asked defiantly.

"Come on, let him go," Derek protested. "He's smaller than you."

"So are you. Both of you," Craig added as an afterthought, though he wasn't totally comfortable anymore. His eyes brightened a little when Joseph and Jude stepped behind him to lend moral support.

Derek felt a tingle run down his back. He didn't care for confrontations, especially not with bullies.

"Why don't you just let the guy go?" Alex said. "You're not proving anything except that you're a jerk, Craig."

Releasing the kid's collar, Craig turned and stepped toward Derek and Alex. "Maybe I'd prove something with you guys, eh? Cliver's a wimp, Alex, and you're weird with all that Hobbit crap you read."

"Live and let live," Alex said.

They continued to stare for a few more seconds, but finally, Craig seemed to decide there was no reason for a fight this morning. He threw up his hand.

"Okay, I let the geek go. Drop it."

Alex gave a slight nod, then he nodded toward Derek and they walked away from the snob cluster.

"You guys better watch yourself, though," Craig called as they made their way back in the direction of Paige. "It's a long summer. Don't make me mad."

"He's just trying to save face," Alex said.

Derek nodded. "Let's just hope he doesn't do it by crushing ours."

Chapter Three

A Summer of Monsters

Derek was introducing Paige and Alex when they heard the squeak of sneakers approaching. He expected to find Craig closing for a new assault, but instead they discovered the kid who'd been attacked walking toward them.

"I wanted to thank you guys," he said, stopping at the edge of the table. "I'm Geoff Novak."

Derek introduced himself and the others.

"I didn't mean to do anything," Geoff said as he sat down in the last vacant chair, apparently assuming he was invited to join them. "I just walked in and got in his way, I guess."

"It doesn't take much to set him off," Alex said. "Who is he?"

"The leader of the in-crowd snobs," Derek said. "The girl you must've looked at wrong is his girlfriend, Amber."

"I thought she was pretty," Geoff said.

"Don't let that mislead you," Derek said. "She's as bad as he is."

"Weird he's so possessive of her," Paige said. "A few minutes ago he was hitting on me."

That made Derek do a double take. He wasn't surprised Paige had caught Craig's attention, but he hadn't realized she'd already encountered the guy.

"What happened?" he asked.

"I was headed for the building, and he pulled up in the parking lot and started coming on to me."

Derek found that a little unsettling. Of course guys like Craig would be after her. Craig wouldn't be the only one, but she had apparently rebuffed the guy.

"I could tell he was trying to be a stud or whatever," she said. "I just kept walking for the building, but before I made it, his girlfriend—what's her name? Amber?—showed up with one of her other friends. It was like I'd done something wrong. I didn't hit on him, he hit on me, but she gave me this look like I'd better watch out."

"Obviously he wouldn't have strayed if you hadn't tempted him," Alex said. "That's the way she sees things."

"Well, that's just great," Paige said. "I've been here an hour, and I've got a cluster of enemies."

"You probably didn't want them as friends anyway," Derek said.

"I can do without them," Geoff agreed.

Derek looked around at the assortment of kids now taking seats at the other tables. Thankfully most of them weren't in the snob category. A lot of girls were on hand, but fewer guys had shown. That wasn't a surprise. A lot of guys wouldn't consider this sort of thing worthy.

A few guys sat at one table, and a few others were sprinkled about among clusters of girls who probably wanted to replace stars on the big screen.

The conversations hushed a few seconds later when a woman walked from stage right up through the rows of tables to take a spot in front of the group.

Miriam Stone had been touted as one of the greatest acting teachers in the universe on the fliers used to promote the class. Derek had doubted that, but now he found himself already impressed. She was more attractive than he had expected, a tall and slender woman with shoulder-length red hair as shiny as woven silk.

She wore dark slacks and a black turtleneck, and her wire-rimmed glasses had octagonal frames. She held a clipboard in the crook of one arm, but a smile crossed her face as she looked over the crowd.

"I have to say, more of you have turned out than I expected," she said. "I guess you all missed the bus for the surfin' excursion."

A couple of kids looked at each other quizzically, and she noted their expressions.

14

"There wasn't really a surfin' excursion," she said, cocking an eyebrow. "Since we're all here, why don't you all write down a little information for me. You'll be signing any children you might have in the future over to the school board."

A light titter rose from the students. They were beginning to catch on to her style. At the snob table, Amber only shook her head and rolled her eyes.

"If you brought paper, take out a sheet and write down your address, shoe size, and your parent's name and Visa card number," Ms. Stone continued. "Not really, okay? Just give me a brief bio about yourself. Knowing yourself is important in acting, so just jot down some pertinent data. If you didn't bring paper, borrow some from your neighbor. I don't think it'll bankrupt anybody. Oh, and put down someone we can contact to send flowers if you get skewered in a sword-fighting scene or anything."

Alex and Derek had brought notebooks. Derek immediately tore out a sheet and offered Paige an extra pen before preparing to write.

"Can I borrow a page, too?" Geoff asked before he could begin.

Derek tried not to let his impatience show. Alex was closer to the kid, but Derek slid his notebook across the table:

"Wow, what's this?" Geoff asked as he flipped the notebook open. Somehow he managed to turn directly to a page where Derek had made notes and a pencil sketch of his monster, which he'd named Ogre.

He felt blood rush to his cheeks as Paige and Alex tilted their heads to get a look at the page.

"It's for a game," he said, a bit embarrassed. Paige would probably think the whole thing was goofy, and Alex would think he was a clod.

"What kind of game?" Geoff persisted.

"Just a thing I saw in a magazine."

Alex reached over and turned the notebook so he could get a better look. "Kind of like a role-playing game?" he asked.

"Kind of," Derek said. "You use monsters instead of heroes."

"Cool," Alex said. "Do you have a group set up?"

"I don't really even have rules yet," Derek said. "I was just bored yesterday and that gave me something to do."

He was looking at Paige, who to his surprise was not recoiling. She seemed interested in the monster as well. He'd usually found that girls considered monsters and anything of the sort stupid.

He was heartened a little when she turned and displayed an expression of curiosity. "You're making monsters?"

"It's from *Scare* magazine," Derek said. "It's a contest." He stammered slightly as he tried to explain.

"I've always liked monster movies," she said. "Have you ever seen the original *Frankenstein*?"

"On cable. It's pretty good."

"So what's your creature like?" she asked.

Derek gave her a quick description of his beast-man.

"Why don't we all enter?" Geoff suggested. "We could see who could come up with the best monster."

"I don't know if it's worth all that trouble," Derek said. "I just did it to kill some time."

"It looks kind of fun," Alex said, cutting off his protest. "You know I've always liked Tolkien and that sort of thing. Your creature reminds me in a way of Gollum, in fact. Only bigger and with more fur."

"He's not as gross as Gollum."

"I think I'd like to make a monster, too," Paige said.

Derek felt his mouth drop open, but he managed to keep his jaw from hitting the table. He never had this kind of luck. She was beautiful and she was interested in something he was. Unbelievable.

"It's not hard," he said, pulling his notebook back to show her notes about the game.

He was about to explain further when Ms. Stone stepped up to their table.

"How are we coming here?" she asked. "Looks like you've jumped past the bio and gone directly to costume design for *Doctor Who*."

"It's a game," Geoff said. "Just a game, that's all. Role playing."

"Oh, well, that's not far removed from what we'll be doing," Ms. Stone said. She blinked. "Go ahead with your bios."

She walked back toward the front of the group, raising her voice to address the whole class again. "While you're finishing up, I'll read you a brief selection from William Blake, 'Tiger, Tiger,'" she said.

16

As she began to read the poem, she captured their attention, however. She was almost transformed as the words began to flow from her lips, mesmerizing the group as she described the tiger. Derek could imagine its striped coat and husky breath as it stalked through the jungle for prey. He was reminded of the old maps he'd seen with the inscription "Here there be tygers!" Maybe literature wasn't that far removed from fun stuff, he thought.

He glanced at Alex, who also seemed transfixed. As she finished the reading, he turned and looked at Derek. "I think I've got my monster," he said. "I think I'll call him Tyger. With a y, you know?"

"I was just thinking that," Derek said.

As the students clapped, Ms. Stone smiled and took a quick bow. "Now you see what reading can do," she said. "Imagination is a powerful tool, and above all this summer we'll be learning to use our imaginations. You can create with your imagination, and that's what acting is all about."

After she'd finished her speech, she explained that the group would be performing scenes from various works of literature, not just plays. She wheeled in a cart of books and let the class spend the rest of the morning looking through the various titles.

There were books of poetry, old plays, collections of short stories, and novels. Derek wound up with a book of British poetry and began to thumb through it while Paige selected a collection of Emily Dickinson. Geoff selected a collection of Victorian ghost stories, while Alex wound up with a couple of books by Langston Hughes and one by Arna Bontemps.

As they sat around their table again, they began to make plans to get together after class. Alex suggested that they gather at his house, which had a large den, the perfect place to plan the game.

They all agreed, and they continued to discuss monster ideas until they happened to look up and notice that Amber had wandered in their direction, probably heading for the restroom to touch up her makeup.

She'd obviously heard their discussion and stopped to eavesdrop. She wrinkled her entire face in revulsion when they looked at her.

"How stupid can you get? Monsters?"

Derek started to raise protest, but Amber shook her head. "When will you people grow up? That's so immature." Her gaze fell on Paige. "I guess some people will put up with anything to be around a bunch of guys."

Paige's eyes flared and her fists clenched into tight balls, but she bit her lip and held any comebacks. "She is such a witch," she said through clenched teeth when Amber had moved on. "Gee, I've only known her an hour, and I can tell I don't like her at all."

"First impressions can be accurate with her," Alex said.

"Yeah, just don't let her get to you," Derek said. "We'll just ignore the snobs. They won't spoil our summer."

"Not at all," Geoff interjected. "It's going to be a summer of monsters. I've got an idea for mine, too."

"Let's get out of here," Alex suggested.

Everyone agreed in unison, and then chairs began to rattle and scrape as the kids got up and started to leave.

"I've got my old heap here," Derek said. "You guys want to ride?"

"Sounds good," Alex said. "You think your Mustang can gallop five blocks?"

"He can limp along," Derek said.

They walked in a group across the asphalt parking lot, and they'd almost reached his vehicle when an eerie sensation struck him. It was almost as if an icy dagger had been jabbed into his back.

He wheeled around, expecting to see a cluster of the snobs smiling smugly. Instead he saw Miriam Stone.

She stood by the gym door with her arms folded. She was watching, watching the class disperse, or was she watching only him? He wasn't sure why, but she made him feel strange.

Chapter Four

The Terror Club

The Jackson den was like a library. Bookshelves lined the walls, and a heavy oak table sat at the center of the room.

"We play cards here sometimes," Alex said as the small group gathered around the table. Outside the sound of distant thunder rumbled. Some clouds had been rolling in as they had driven toward the house, but now an afternoon thunderstorm seemed imminent.

"Guess the weather will be right for this sort of thing," Paige said.

"Really," Derek agreed.

Alex had collected notepads and pens for the others, and they sat for a while looking at each other, trying to come up with creatures.

"We don't want to do just movie monsters," Geoff said, tapping his notepad with his pen. "That'd never win the contest, and it wouldn't be that much fun for us either."

"I was going to make a vampire," Paige said. "I always liked reading Anne Rice."

"Anybody could come up with a vampire," Geoff protested. "Or a werewolf. Or a mummy. Let's rule those out." His voice rose a little as he spoke, and while he didn't seem angry, he was adamant.

"I guess he's got a good point," Alex said. "All of those standard monsters have been overdone."

"What is your monster going to be like?" Paige asked Geoff.

"It's really lean and thin," he said, his eyes widening as he spoke. "The legs are long and, like, double-jointed, so it can jump. They're almost like spider legs, but more muscular. And it has long arms, too, so it can reach out and claw things. Or it can, like, get up the sides of buildings and stuff. It's, what would you call it, wiry?"

Derek had to hand it to him. He'd come up with a different approach. It was not a huge hulking monster, but it still sounded creepy.

"It's fast, too, and it has big round eyes, and its head is kind of shaped like a cat's head. The ears are pointed so it can hear for long distances, too, and there's a strong sense of smell so it can track its prey, and the fangs are like a cat's fangs, too. Long and needle-sharp. He's got whiskers, too, like a cat. They're sensitive, they help him sense things also."

"Ooooo," Paige said, rubbing her arms. "That is pretty ghastly. You're just coming up with this off the top of your head?"

"I've been thinking about it all morning," Geoff said, writing down some of his ideas. "Since it's catlike I'm going to call it The Feline."

It was definitely not something he wanted to encounter in a dark alley, Derek decided.

As he considered the monster, the sound of the thunder rumbled again, closer this time.

"Okay where do I start?" Paige asked. "Talk me through this."

"What are you scared of?" Geoff asked. "That's what will make it the most frightening."

"I've never really thought about it," Paige said. "I guess I'm scared by the usual things like we were talking about, vampires, werewolves …"

"What else?" Geoff asked. "What have you had nightmares about?"

She rolled her eyes, brown eyes that almost made Derek's head feel as if it were floating as he watched her.

"I guess I'm scared of, of, I don't know, spooky things, things that can sneak up on you, things that are ghostly."

"We're not dealing with ghosts here," Geoff said, on the verge of getting annoyed.

More thunder sounded, and then the rain began. They could hear it on the leaves outside, and it splattered against the window.

"It's really coming down," Alex said. "That's summer weather for you."

He was about to get up to look out the window when the lights went out, plunging the room into darkness. Thick draperies were pulled closed over the window, so almost no light at all was available.

"I'll get candles," Alex said.

"Do it quick," Paige suggested.

Derek considered reaching for her hand but decided against it. He'd only known her since this morning, and she might think he was being too forward.

"This should at least get everybody's imagination going," Geoff said. "We should have thought of this anyway."

"Right," Alex said from across the room. The sound of his leg crashing into something solid followed.

"That hurt," he said. "Just in case anyone was wondering."

A few seconds later a closet door opened, and he could be heard fumbling around. He seemed to be shoving things aside, and finally a match flared, forming a small oval of orange which encompassed him in its glow. He looked like a ghostly presence as he touched the flame to a candlewick.

"These are old Christmas candles," he said, returning to the table and lighting another candle once he was seated.

The golden flame did not expel the darkness. It only chased the shadows back, and as the flame flickered, the walls around them seemed to dance.

"Sure you want to keep this up now?" Alex asked.

"It's perfect," Geoff said. "You decided what you're afraid of yet, Paige?"

"Yeah, the dark."

"Things that go bump in the night?" Alex asked. "The unknown," Paige said.

"What about something that's intangible like that," Derek suggested. "Smoke, fog, mist .. ."

"A mist creature," Paige said brightly. "That's different."

Geoff considered it for a moment. "It is," he agreed. "Something that doesn't really have form. It could move silently."

"It could be there and nobody would know it," Paige added. "It could linger, and people would think it was like part of the fog."

"That's good," Geoff said. "What else could it do?"

"Suck the life out of people?" Paige suggested, wrinkling her nose at the prospect.

"Nah," Geoff said. "That's old hat."

"Well, let's see," Paige said, rolling her eyes upward as she tried to come up with an idea. "Smoke smothers."

"That's kinda mundane, too," Geoff said. "What else could it do?"

"Maybe it could affect people emotionally," Derek suggested. "Making them scared, or angry."

"How about if it takes whatever a person's feeling and makes it so intense that they can't stand it?" Paige asked. "That's unique. It could do that to subdue the person, then smother."

Geoff pursed his lips as he considered the final suggestion. After a moment, he nodded. "That ought to work. Can it do anything else?"

"Maybe each person it gets to makes it stronger," she said. "And the stronger it gets, the harder it is to fight it."

"Put all that in," Geoff said. "If you have to pit it against other monsters, that could be helpful. Boy, if the other kids just come up with werewolves and vampires, we should do really well."

Bending over the paper, Paige wrote a brief description of what they had discussed. Her handwriting was precise and elegant. Derek watched her ponytail bobbing slightly as she worked, some candlelight shining on the strands. She looked like a model.

"Okay, her name is Vapor," she said when she was finished. She pushed the paper forward for Geoff and then Derek and Alex to look over.

"It looks good," Geoff said.

Derek nodded in agreement. "You're a good monster maker," he said, feeling good about a chance to offer a compliment.

"Thanks," she beamed back.

The smile convinced Derek they'd have to find a way to spend some time together this summer, time besides the workshop and playing this game. They could have fun. Playing the game would be fine, but he didn't want that to consume all the days.

"Now me?" Alex asked.

"Yeah, your tiger creature," Geoff agreed. "What's he like?"

"He's bigger than a normal Bengal tiger," Alex said, "and more mysterious. He's a culmination of all the legends, a massive creature that hunts at night. He has glowing green eyes and sharp claws."

'We don't want him to be routine," Geoff warned. He grasped one of the candles and moved it closer to Alex so that he could see his notepad better.

"He can see at night, can smell, can devour with his powerful jaws."

"Good," Geoff said. "And he also is protected by magic energy. How's that?"

"That's great," Alex said, making more notes.

After a few more minutes of discussion, he finalized his description and placed his pen on the table. "All done."

"We'd better get these in the mail once the rain stops," Geoff suggested. "The sooner we get them off, the sooner we'll know if we're winners."

"I'll have to find some envelopes," Alex said. He took one of the candles and walked across the room, leaving the others at the table.

Paige folded her arms under her breasts and shivered. "I think this is getting wild," she said. "I hope we do get responses so we can start playing. I've never been excited by the D&D thing, but this sounds like it'll be something I can get into."

Derek nodded. He was focused more on her than the game. In the candle's glow she was like a vision from a dream. She looked like a fair maiden, and he imagined her wearing an elegant medieval gown, sitting in some candlelit dining room, her lips slightly parted as her eyes reflected the flickering light. She was—

"We're just a mad bunch of monster makers," Geoff said, shattering the daydream.

"Yeah, we are," Derek said curtly, looking over at Geoff. His remark had been so geeky he wondered if he should've let Craig have him. Too much fervor could get annoying quickly. Derek glanced next to Paige, who was smiling and shaking her head. They were in agreement. Geoff was a little immature.

The door rattled open then, making all of them jump as Alex returned. "I scared up some envelopes," he said. "Do you remember the address?"

"It's pretty basic," Derek said. He recited the address from memory.

Dutifully, Paige took one of the envelopes and addressed it, then folded her monster description and stuffed it inside. She licked the flap quickly, wincing at the taste of the glue.

Derek was wondering how they could find some way to get some time away from Geoff. He was the kind of guy who bubbled with a little too much enthusiasm about everything and had a strong potential to cling if he wasn't kept in check. If Derek offered to drive her to the post office, Geoff would want a ride as well. There might be no chances, but he suggested the ride anyway.

"The rain will be letting up soon," he said.

"Yeah, and I need to be getting home," she agreed. "Can you drop me there?"

"Sure."

He waited for Derek to request a ride also, but he kept silent as Alex went to the window and spread open the curtains. The rain had stopped, and some sunshine was already beginning to appear.

"These storms never last that long," Alex said.

'Weird how fast that one blew over," Paige said. "Almost like it coincided with our little endeavor here. Scary."

Alex raised his index finger and shook it. "Now, now. Don't start taking this all too seriously. It's just a game."

"Right, just a game," Geoff echoed.

"Yeah, well, we'll be on the lookout for monsters just the same," Derek joked.

"Yeah," Paige said. "They could be anywhere."

"Under the table?" Geoff asked. "In the closet. In the sugar bowl. Even in the toilet tank." He began to snicker.

Paige rolled her eyes, and again, Derek and Alex had to shake their heads.

He was trying far too hard to be funny and to be accepted. Maybe he'd get better and quit trying so hard once he figured out he wasn't going to be rejected by the group. Unless he didn't learn soon when it was time to shut up.

Chapter Five

Nightmare Forest

The snobs were gathered in the parking lot the next morning before class, leaning against a couple of cars. Not their cars, of course. They wouldn't want to scratch their paint jobs. They'd selected some vehicles parked near the gym's rear door.

As Derek pulled into the lot, he noticed them and shook his head with contempt. "I was hoping they would've decided the workshop wasn't their kind of fun," he told Paige, who was sitting in his passenger seat. And looking as beautiful as the day before in denim shorts, a violet-colored long-sleeve pullover, and black hightops with white socks.

When he'd dropped her at her house the previous day, he'd offered her a ride for this morning. He'd been surprised when she'd accepted. He was almost ready to let himself believe she might like him. She'd been hanging around with him for a day, she was supposed to let him show her around, and she was going to play the monster game.

What more could he want?

Despite all those positive signs, he never allowed himself to get too optimistic about life and especially not girls. Craig had come on to her, after all. If she could get the attention of one of the football stars, what kind of chance did he stand?

He found a parking place at the edge of the building, wishing there were an easier way to get inside. The snobs had formed a gauntlet so that anyone coming in from the parking lot would have to walk past them.

The only other way would be to walk all the way around the building, and he couldn't do that. It would look bad in front of Paige.

He wasn't sure if Craig would try something or not, but he decided to be ready. He didn't know how he'd hold up against the bigger boy. When he considered that, he felt skinnier than ever, but he'd do his best if it came to that.

"Ready?" he asked as he killed the engine.

"Sure," Paige said. The smile she flashed made him forget all about his problems.

For a second anyway. They walked side by side around the corner and along the sidewalk toward the back door. He felt the short hairs on the back of his neck stand up as he moved, but he didn't look toward the snobs.

He could hear them laughing, and he immediately imagined their giggles were directed at him, but he didn't let himself think about what they were saying.

As he and Paige walked past, they raised their voices. The tone was at one of those mawkish levels designed to be heard.

"Can you believe what she's wearing?" Suzi asked. "That is sooo tacky."

From the corner of his eye, Derek looked at Paige. She'd heard the remark, and he could see in her eyes that it had hurt her feelings. She didn't react, though. She just kept staring straight ahead.

"What can you expect?" Amber asked with a heavy sigh, obviously annoyed that the remark hadn't generated a more visible response. "I don't know what her daddy does, but I hope he finds steady work soon."

Paige bit her lip. The remark had cut, but she tried to hide it and moved on.

"She doesn't have very good taste in men," Craig added, slugging Jude on the shoulder.

Jude didn't care for that much, but he nodded and smiled, keeping up the party line.

"Just ignore them," Derek whispered.

"I'm trying," Paige said. "But it's like ignoring athlete's foot."

"I know."

They continued toward the door, which seemed to be a mile away.

"I wish she'd do something with all that hair," Suzi added. "I mean, what does she think? Is she trying to be like Mariah Carey or something?"

Derek almost wheeled around at that crack, but Paige's hand shot over and touched his arm. "It's not worth it," she whispered from the corner of her mouth.

They kept moving. Derek's back almost felt as if it were stinging as jokes and laughter continued. When they finally reached the door, he grasped the handle and yanked it open so that Paige could step inside.

"Sorry about all that. Part of it is because you're new, and part of it's because we stood up to Craig yesterday."

"It's okay. I'm glad you didn't get into anything with them. They're not worth it. They're just petty dweebs who feel good about themselves by tearing other people down."

"Yeah, I know it," Derek said. "Let's just find Alex and Geoff and forget about them. And by the way, I think your outfit looks great."

He felt almost silly uttering the compliment, but her smile made him sure he'd said the right thing. "Thanks," she said. "It's nothing they'd wear, but I'm comfortable."

They continued across the gym, locating Alex who had already taken his seat at their table.

"How's it going?" he asked.

"We just met a few people we'd like to feed to some monsters," Paige said. "Otherwise it's going fine."

After a class period in which they got to try some preliminary readings with only a few snickers from the snob table, Derek and Paige decided on hamburgers for lunch. Again he was surprised she wanted to hang around with him, but he didn't complain.

He recommended The Petitt Burger. The name was a play on words, since the burgers were promised to be biggest in town. They were also acclaimed as the best burgers in town, and as far as Derek could tell that was true.

After they'd ordered, they sat back in their booth in the darkened dining room and ignored the sounds from the kitchen and other tables.

"I can't quit thinking about those jerks this morning," Paige said.

"They're always like that," Derek said as he unfolded his napkin and spread it across his jeans. "Somebody ought to do something about them."

"Yeah, you're right."

"Sorry I brought them up," she said, brightening. "Why don't you tell me about town? I don't know much about the area."

As briefly as he could, Derek outlined what he knew of Pembrook's history. It had actually grown from a small town that had been established just before the Civil War. He'd learned that in eighth-grade history. Nobody got out of eighth grade without an intensive study of Pembrook's past.

The conversation soon departed from the past, however. They laughed and talked for a while about CDs and movies they liked, and then their meals were delivered.

As they started to eat, more-pressing matters came to mind. Derek felt himself growing nervous as he began to consider asking Paige to go to a movie on the weekend. That seemed to be the next step.

His mom would be paid on Friday, so she would give him his allowance. Money wouldn't be a problem even though he didn't have a job this summer, but sitting here across the table from her, laughing with her, he found the idea of asking Paige for a formal date almost frightening.

What if she didn't want to be more than a buddy?

Or what if she just didn't like him enough. That might make the whole summer awkward, at least when he was around her.

The easy way would be to pal around with her. He wouldn't have to worry about messing things up that way, but he liked her. He was discovering he liked her a lot—the way she smiled, the way she turned her head, her jokes, her stories. He'd never thought he could be so charmed, but in just a couple of days he was almost lightheaded.

As she sipped her soft drink, he put down his sandwich and placed his hands on the table in front of him. "You know, there's a new comedy opening this weekend."

"Really?" She arched her eyebrows, but she didn't go any further.

"I thought, uh, you know ..." He cleared his throat and looked directly into her eyes. "You might like to go."

She laughed and reached across the table to touch his arm. "That would be great."

Derek wanted to jump out of his chair. She'd said Yes! His heart seemed to flutter as the realization settled over him. Yes! A date, a real date, not just bumming around together or hanging out with Geoff and Alex.

He almost wondered if he was imagining the whole thing as she smiled at him. She was so pretty, so wonderful, and she was going to go out with him.

He had forgotten all about his hamburger and might not have picked it up again if she hadn't reminded him of it with a nod and a knowing smile that formed her dimples. He almost felt stupid as he looked down at his plate, but he recovered his senses and picked it up again.

They were still laughing and talking a little while later when Geoff found them. Alex was with him, and they tapped on the window and waved first, then made their way to the front door.

Derek found he didn't mind if they sat down now. He and Paige would have time together later, so there was no need to worry about having friends around.

Not even Geoff in an excited mode. "We've been talking about our monsters," Geoff said. "We've got lots of possibilities."

"I mentioned role-playing games I'd played," Alex said as an explanation for Geoff's enthused state.

"This can be better than any of those," Geoff said. He didn't really seem to be speaking to anyone in the room. His eyes were wide, and he was excited. "We can come up with the greatest role-playing game ever."

Paige pursed her lips to mask a grin as he continued. He was almost like a carnival barker, hailing the virtues of his role-playing game.

Alex also had to lift his eyebrows. Derek nodded back.

The poor guy had probably never had many friends, and locating a handful with at least some similar interest was apparently overwhelming. Derek could identify to a point, although he'd probably never been as much of an outcast as Geoff.

"I think we should make up our own game instead of waiting on *Scare*," Geoff said.

He raised his hands, making a broad gesture of dismissal. "Who needs the magazine? We've got our own imaginations." He raised a finger to his temple. "We can come up with a better game than a bunch of burned-out magazine editors."

"It's not that big a deal," Alex said. "We can get the stuff from the magazine."

"We don't need them," Geoff insisted. He still sounded like a barker. "All we need is our own imagination, and we'll go from there. We'll make maps, and we'll make monsters. Great monsters!"

Derek checked Paige's face to see how she felt about the suggestion. She gave a quick expression that suggested it would be fine with her.

Alex also seemed agreeable to the idea, so Derek nodded. "Maybe it's something we can check out."

"Yeah, what we need is an environment for it," Geoff added. "I know there's that wooded area, you know the one I mean?"

"That wooded area at the corner of Wayne Street? It's supposed to be haunted," Derek said. "I was thinking more in terms of maybe a kitchen-table game. A few of us sitting around a board or map or whatever."

"That'd be like a bridge club," Geoff protested. "This is a 'Terror Club.' We should have a realistic setting that's spooky, and a haunted wood would be perfect. We could map it out and that would be the environment for the game when we do sit at a table to play."

Derek leaned back. He didn't really have a problem with the wood. He'd strolled the outer edges a few times, but he had no idea how deep it would be, or what perils might wait there. This was summer. Snakes would be out, not to mention things like fleas or ticks, which would make monsters seem mild by comparison.

"What does everyone else think?" he asked.

"It couldn't be that bad, could it?" Paige asked. "As long as we're careful, it could be a fun place."

"I don't think it would be that bad," Alex agreed. "It'll be hot, but the trees will make it shady."

"Just a scouting expedition," Geoff said. "We'll just look around."

"Okay," Derek said at last. "It's a mission."

He dragged some bills out of his jeans and paid for the burgers, and then their entire band headed out to Derek's car.

30

When he pulled to a stop at the edge of the wood, and they all piled out of the Mustang, the afternoon sun had reached its scorching point. Even the breeze that whispered through the leaves didn't do much to cool things off.

"I've thought about walking through there," Alex said, looking back through the trees. "It's not really what I'd call scary"

"What's the story on the haunting?" Paige asked. "Is there really supposed to be a ghost?"

"I've never heard anything specific," Derek said. "It's a wooded area in the middle of a residential section, though when I was a kid there was a rumor that a cemetery was back in there somewhere."

"Makes you wonder why they never cleared it," Alex said. "That could be the source of the legends, a forgotten graveyard. Scary"

Geoff reached into his pocket and pulled out a small notebook.

"Well, let's check it out," he said. "We can figure out what it's got to offer."

He left the road's shoulder and began to step through the tall grass, scribbling notes as he moved.

Alex and Derek looked at each other, shrugged, and followed with Paige not far behind.

"If we see any snakes, you guys can carry me out," she suggested.

"If we see any snakes, we'll be flying out of here," Alex said.

As they moved beneath the oak and pine trees, the shade provided a little relief from the sun, and in the shadows the grass was not thick. That made movement easier, so Geoff quickly picked up his pace, leading them on a winding route that dodged underbrush and brambles.

"It is sort of scary," Paige said, nodding toward the shadows created by the intertwining branches high above their heads. The tree limbs formed what was almost a ceiling, hiding much of the sky as they moved deeper.

"Monsters could hide back in here," Geoff said, indicating the nooks and crannies of the forest. "And my monster could climb around on all these trees easy. So this would be the Monster Wood," Derek said. "In a game environment."

"Yeah, or maybe something catchier, Geoff suggested. "Nightmare Forest."

"It's not that bad," Paige said, though she shuddered when a branch brushed against her shoulder.

"Maybe we could play out here at night," Geoff suggested. "That could really be great."

"I don't know about that," Derek protested. He wasn't sure if anyone wanted to go that far. He wasn't worried about monsters, but it would be easy to get lost out here in the dark, or hurt.

"Come on," Geoff said. "Anybody can play in the daylight, but at night it would really be great."

"We'll see. We haven't even got a real idea of how to play," Derek said.

"We'll get one soon, though. Or who knows? Maybe we'll hear from the magazine soon."

"It could be fun," Alex said. "In an offbeat sort of way."

Derek looked around. He didn't really feel like a leader of the group, but the others seemed to have started looking to him or questioning him for approval, since the game more or less stemmed from him.

"Well, we'd need to have a really good idea of the area," he said. "If we played for real. We don't want to get lost out here, and I think it'd be better if we played on maps for a while first."

"I'll work on a map," Geoff suggested. "Let's keep going."

Pushing forward they made their way through a tangle of vines and worked on around another cluster of trees. Geoff continued to scribble notes and make other markings in his notebook.

"Will you be able to do any good with that once we're out of here?" Alex asked. "Since you seem to be our official cartographer."

"I'm pretty good," Geoff said. "And I have a good memory. I'll work on a map for each of us. A map'll be important for the game anyway."

"You've got to have a map for D&D or anything," Alex agreed.

Derek nodded in agreement with both of them. They both had good points, and as long as everyone stayed levelheaded the game should be okay.

He helped Geoff clear some thick bush aside so that they would move forward, and in a few moments progress became a little easier.

After moving still further, they found a branch that had been broken, as if perhaps someone had passed this way. He wondered if they had found what had once been a trail, or maybe even a road. The trees were not quite as close together. Maybe there was something back here to which people had once traveled.

Continuing onward, they rounded a stand of oaks, and as they looked forward, they all froze in their tracks.

About a hundred yards ahead, overgrown and shadowed by overhanging branches, was a small cemetery. It was bordered by a wrought-iron fence which had long ago begun to rust, and the gate, while padlocked, hung loose from its hinges.

Geoff was the first to break the silence with an exclamation. "You were right!" he said, bumping his hand against Derek's arm. "There really is a graveyard back here."

Derek felt Paige brushing nervously against his other arm. He wished the circumstances for that touch were different.

"Now this is scary," Paige said. "Look at the old monuments."

Towers of gray stone jutted up beyond the fence. They were badly weathered, but at least a vestige of their past grandeur remained.

"This really does make it a Nightmare Wood," Geoff said. He was about to step forward when the branches above his head suddenly rattled loudly.

He looked up and let out a quick yowl.

Chapter Six

"What does he care about monsters?"

Geoff brought his arm up just in time to deflect the attack of the bird that was winging toward him. As it brushed against his sleeve, the dark-feathered creature squawked and then beat its wings swiftly, disappearing back into the concealing leaves.

Paige placed a hand over her heart and breathed a quick sigh. "I could've done without that," she said.

"Wonder why it swooped down like that?" Alex asked.

"Maybe it has a nest nearby or something," Geoff said, quickly checking his arm to make sure he hadn't been scratched by a beak or claw. He seemed to be okay.

"Well, are we going to have a look at the cemetery or what?" he asked.

Everyone seemed hesitant, as if the prospect of setting foot inside the old cemetery was more frightening than they wanted to consider, but finally Derek nodded. It couldn't be that bad, especially in daylight, and they'd already come this far.

"Let's do it," he said.

Slowly they moved forward, sticking close together, moving almost as a single entity. The grass, dried by the summer heat, crunched and crackled under their footsteps, as if it were shouting warnings about proceeding.

When they reached the gate, Derek realized he was sweating more from nerves than from the heat—his skin felt hot, and his heart was pounding.

Together, he and Alex grasped the bars on one of the two gate doors, twisting sideways enough to make an opening where it was separated from its hinge on one side.

"Who goes first?" Paige asked once they were ready to proceed.

They found themselves looking at each other. No one was really keen on the idea, but Derek again felt the tension of leadership. "I will," he said, almost reluctantly.

'Turning to the gate, he stooped slightly and slid through the hole. The others followed while he stood looking across the rows of headstones.

They were gray and cracked, and they jutted up from the ground almost like rows of buildings. All the graves in the cemetery where his father had been buried—the only other cemetery he'd visited—had featured flat headstones. That was supposed to make it easier for mowing.

That wasn't a problem here. No one had ever tried to mow this place. It was overgrown with weeds and brush, and mold had climbed across many of the markers, coloring the stone a greenish shade.

He felt Paige touching his arm as she came to his side. She didn't grip him tightly, but he could tell she was afraid.

"It's just a cemetery," she said, as if she was trying most of all to convince herself.

"A really cool one," Geoff said. "Look at those headstones."

He pointed toward a couple of markers that pointed skyward like castle towers, and beyond those were more tall stones almost like pillars. Past those was another headstone, wide and crafted with an ornate rose design.

"Man, could you imagine this place at midnight on a full moon?" Geoff asked.

"I'd rather not," Paige admitted. She knelt in front of one of the headstones, then looked at another.

"They all died around 1893," she said. "And look, look at all of them. They were all teenagers, at least on this row."

Derek and Alex quickly checked stones on other rows.

"They're almost all that way," Alex said. "There must have been a malaria outbreak or something. You know they didn't realize mosquitoes caused that until, like, 1900."

"Wow," Derek said. "That's weird."

"That's in the past. It'd be great for the game," Geoff said.

"I don't think so," Paige said.

"We don't have to be here to play the game," Derek said. "Just get the lay of it, and I'm sure our imaginations will serve us when we play in a nice quiet living room."

"Okay," Geoff said with a heavy sigh of aggravation. He took out the old-fashioned fountain pen which he had returned to his pocket and began to make notes and quick sketches of the headstones.

While the graveyard covered only a couple of acres, it seemed almost endless, the underbrush and tangled weeds and vines contributing to the illusion. Making the way to the rear fence meant weaving around dozens of headstones.

When they finally traversed the array of graves, Paige noticed the dilapidated old cabin, which sagged in the rear corner of the cemetery

The gray wood planks from which it had been constructed had been faded by ages of weather and wear, and rust covered the old tin roof.

"Must've been a caretaker's shack," Alex speculated as they moved toward the narrow porch in front.

Dingy shutters had been closed over the windows, and a rusted screen hung over the cracked and peeling front door.

"It's spookier than the graves," Paige observed.

"Probably about ready to fall down," Derek added. "Obviously this place hasn't had a caretaker in years."

The place didn't catch Geoff's interest. He turned from it quickly and continued to sketch some of the headstones.

"Can we go yet?" Paige asked as he finished shaping a small stone.

"I guess so," he said, and got no disagreement from Alex or Derek.

Making a quicker trip back across the cemetery, the group squeezed through the gate and started back along the trail they had come, easing into the thick shadows offered by the trees.

Derek thought he heard some movement behind them as they traipsed back along their almost-nonexistent trail, but he didn't allow his suspicions to progress. It was probably only the bird again, or a squirrel or some other normal woodland animal, not a monster. There was no need to get skittish just because the wood was a bit eerie. That was all imaginary.

When they reached the roadway again, they stood talking for a few more minutes. Then Alex decided to walk the short distance to his house.

"You want to tag along with me?" he asked Geoff. "Do you live in my direction?"

Geoff shook his head. "No, no. My house is the other way."

"We ought to drop by to see you for the game sometime," Paige suggested politely. "You deserve a home-court advantage like all of us."

"I can win anyway," Geoff said, as if her joke might have offended him a little. He smiled a second later, however. "Actually we're not really settled in yet. My mom won't allow company till everything's spotless."

"Whatever," Paige said. She gave him a wave as he struck off in one direction. Alex waved also and headed away as well.

"I hope you don't mind the Terror Club and everything," Derek said as he and Paige climbed into his car.

"It breaks up the monotony," she said. "I know people who'd say it was goofy, but I like to do things that stimulate my imagination."

"I do, too," Derek agreed. "I guess that's why I got interested in it in the first place."

"The workshop should be the same as we go on," she said.

"Maybe. We can always drop out if it gets too boring, or if the snobs get to be too much of a hassle."

He felt as if his chest were filled with helium as they rode. He was almost floating, just having her near, and he hoped she was feeling the same. There seemed to be a twinkle in her eye that suggested the affirmative to that question.

"You know, when my parents told me we'd be moving, I almost cried," she said as they moved up a cross street that would eventually wind toward her house. "It's tough to change horses in midstream, or whatever, but having you around helps with the transition."

"Thanks," he said softly. "So you didn't want to come here?"

"I didn't even know where Pembrook was, and I didn't like the idea of leaving all my friends."

"I was kind of young when my dad died. That's when we moved. It took me a while to adjust, to not having Dad and to not knowing anybody."

"I had a lot of friends," Paige said. "No steady boyfriend, though."

Derek wasn't sure how to react to that remark. Was he a boyfriend? No, he decided, they hadn't even gone out yet. He couldn't be considered a boyfriend, but maybe things were heading in that direction.

Slowly, he followed the roadway around a curve that bordered a vacant lot almost as overgrown as the wood. He looked through the trees as a light breeze drifted through the air.

Leaves fluttered, and birds chirped, and he thought he saw movement somewhere beyond a growth of shrubs. He slowed, squinting against the afternoon sun that glared on the car window as he tried to see what it was. He couldn't make out anything.

"What is it?" Paige asked.

"I don't know. The wind," he said with a laugh to conceal the sudden feeling of apprehension that had struck him. Imagination was plaguing him again. Nothing more, nothing to be worried about.

This silly "Terror Club" thing was making him paranoid. Why should he be watching the shadows just because they'd made up a few monsters? If that was all that it took to make monsters, the world would be overrun with them. News reports would be like *Night of the Living Dead*, which he'd watched a few months back on cable.

The Terror Club was only a game. No need to watch for ogres or tyger-creatures nor to worry about the dead from the old cemetery.

––––––––

As they traveled on, he felt venturesome since he'd convinced himself there were no monsters, and at last he let his hand slide along the seat to take Paige's hand. She didn't resist. In fact, she gave his hand a slight squeeze, an assurance that she didn't mind and that she liked him, too.

"I don't feel as lonely here as I thought I would," she said.

He smiled as he eased the car slowly to her driveway. Reluctantly he climbed out and walked her to the front door. "You want to come in?"

"Well, my mom did leave some chores for me," he said. "But I'll see you in the morning."

"Okay. I'll look forward to it."

She gave his cheek a quick peck just before spinning and going inside. He stood there several seconds after the door had closed, feeling like floating again. He hadn't expected that, but it was wonderful.

By late afternoon, Derek had done most of the things his mom had requested in straightening up the house, a task he had undertaken primarily because he would need her cooperation and monetary assistance if he was going out with Paige this weekend. He'd had a job and had saved some money during the school year, but the store he had worked had gone out of business just before summer vacation.

He was sitting in the living room looking over the book from class when he heard the car in the driveway. He got up and went to the window and was a bit disappointed when he saw the vehicle that belonged to Neil pulling into the driveway behind his mom's vehicle.

Derek knew his mom seemed more and more serious about Neil lately. He had always known his mom might marry again someday, but he wasn't sure he wanted it to be to Neil. There must be some guy out there who wasn't so darned perfect. Neil had perfect hair, perfect clothes. He'd probably been like the snobs when he'd been younger. Derek would've liked his mom to find someone a little more creative, and someone who didn't want to be so fatherly.

Both his mom and Neil climbed out of the cars, and he saw Neil was carrying a shopping bag from the local Chinese take-out. He was staying for dinner!

Derek would have to be polite to him all evening or risk making his mother angry. That was almost too large a challenge, but for Paige he could endure it.

He put on a smile, at least as much of a smile as he could manage, as he greeted them at the front door.

"How you doing, dude?" Neil asked as he stepped across the threshold.

"Okay," Derek managed.

"Help Neil with the Chinese food," Mrs. Cliver suggested. "He's walking wounded."

Derek looked at Neil's hand which was wrapped in a bandage.

"What happened?"

39

"Cut it on some office equipment at work," Neil said. "I've got to stay away from paper shredders."

Derek took the shopping bag, though Neil seemed to be managing all right. "It's a mere flesh wound," he quipped. Derek didn't laugh.

They set up dinner at the kitchen table, and Derek couldn't complain about the selection. Mr. Lee's Oriental Garden had the best Chinese food in the state, and Neil and Mom had selected a variety of some of the best dishes. Spooning the food onto plates, they began to eat, savoring the flavor.

"So your mom tells me you've signed up for a drama course," Neil said as Derek devoured some Mongolian beef.

"Sort of," Derek said. "It's a reading workshop. We don't actually do plays yet. We study literature by reading it. We haven't really gotten into it yet, but I think it'll be more fun than looking for DHMs."

"DHMs?" Neil asked.

"Deep hidden meanings," Mrs. Cliver translated.

"You remember looking for themes and messages in stories."

"Oh yeah," Neil said. "I'd forgotten. So, Derek, it's a new teacher?"

"Apparently she just moved to town. She's a bit odd, but not too bad."

"I'm-sure she's good."

Dinner passed almost painlessly with a continuation of the conversation – Neil asking polite questions to feign interest and Derek answering with as much courtesy as he could muster.

After dinner, while his mom puttered around in the kitchen, Neil and Derek retired to the living room for television. *The Simpsons* was a rerun, but they watched anyway. Derek suspected this whole situation was a setup to get him more accustomed to Neil. He willed himself to be calm.

During a commercial break, Neil got up for coffee, and when he returned, his leg brushed Derek's notepad to the floor.

It fluttered open to a new picture of Ogre.

"That's a fierce-looking fellow," Neil said, placing the tablet back on the coffee table.

"It's for a club, sort of," Derek said. He almost had the explanation about the Terror Club memorized now. He rattled it off as briefly as possible.

"Whooo. Scary," Neil said with a mock shudder. Then he asked a few more questions that didn't seem to be solely to pretend interest.

What does he care about monsters? Derek wondered to himself.

Maybe Neil had a little more of an imagination than he'd been giving him credit for. Maybe Neil wasn't a total creep.

Or maybe he was pretending interest in a new effort to make Derek his pal.

He gave a brief answer to Neil's questions, but he didn't lead into further discussion about the game. Interested or not, Neil was probably a little old for monster making.

Wasn't he?

Chapter Seven

King of the Nightmare Wood

The next morning, Derek found Paige and Alex quickly as people began to gather for the workshop. Kids were clomping onto the stage and laughing as they assembled at their tables, and the sound carried across the gym in a cacophony.

"Almost all the monster makers in one place," Alex said with a chuckle.

Derek laughed as well and shook his head. "Let's try to keep it in perspective," he said.

"I'm trying," Alex said as they walked across the gym. "Geoff, on the other hand ..."

"Takes it very seriously," Derek said.

"Extremely seriously. I thought he was going to pop a blood vessel or something."

They both began to laugh, almost doubling over until Paige put up her hand to stop them. She was on the verge of giggling, but as she fought to keep the corners of her mouth from turning up she gave them a stern stare.

"Come on," she warned. "It's just something the poor guy likes. Let him enjoy it. You guys don't want to start sounding like the snobs, do you?"

That was a sobering thought. Alex and Derek wiped the smiles off their faces and managed to remain serious for a second before bursting into laughter again.

"You guys are terrible," Paige said, spinning and walking away from them. They looked at each other for a second and then rushed to catch up with her.

The trio was already seated when Geoff arrived with a large piece of paper rolled under his arm. He began unrolling it almost before he was in his chair.

"I've got an environment worked out," he said. "I incorporated the neighborhoods and the Nightmare Wood, too. We could really start playing any time."

He was so sincere that they almost broke into laughter again, but they managed to stifle themselves. They didn't want to hurt his feelings, Derek reminded himself.

As the paper unfurled, Derek recognized an almost-exact duplicate of their edge of Pembrook, drawn in pencil—each street was there and Geoff had done a detailed sketch of the Nightmare Wood with indications of the trees and a blocked-off region for the cemetery.

"You must've been up all night," Derek said. Geoff shrugged. "It was worth it."

"Well, you did a good job," Paige said.

"Really," Alex agreed, turning the paper slightly so that he could get a better look at it. "This is looking great, just like a professional job. I'm getting excited to play this."

"Yeah," Paige said. "We can forget about *Scare* all together."

"Well, the magazine inspired it," Geoff said. "If Derek hadn't read the ad, we never would have come up with the idea."

"Whoa, now we've got a game with monsters running all over Pembrook," Alex noted. "Scary stuff."

He was bending forward to pick out his own street on the map when Craig and Joseph approached, the bustle of the other kids muffling their movements. They seemed to materialize at the edge of the table. Derek almost jumped when he realized they were there.

"What have we got here?" Craig asked. "You guys planning some kind of revolution? You going to overthrow the mayor and put geeks in charge of Pembrook?"

"Nothing like that," Paige said curtly. "It's just a game."

Joseph turned his head for a better look at the map. "Looks like Pembrook to me."

"It's an environment for our role-playing game," Derek said, trying to sound matter-of-fact, as if he didn't realize they were being sarcastic.

"Are you guys going to be elves or something?" Craig asked.

"It's more of a horror game than a swords-and-sorcery game," Alex said. "We got the idea from a magazine. We'll be using monsters as our player-characters."

"Monsters, ooh," Craig said. He then tapped Joseph's arm. "We better watch out. These guys are going to be sending monsters out."

"Right," Joseph said. "Geek monsters."

They laughed as they turned and headed for their own table.

Geoff had turned a bright red, and his gaze was locked on them. His eyes were almost bulging out of their sockets, and Derek could see the muscle in his jaw twitching.

Anger was boiling inside Geoff, so much so that he was trembling. Paige glanced at him, bit her lip, and looked at Derek.

Alex reached over and touched Geoff's shoulder. For a second Geoff didn't notice. He was too consumed by his anger.

Only after a second did he respond to Alex, and an instant later he shook his head, snapping back to reality. He seemed a bit embarrassed, and he gave a weak smile. "They just made me crazy for a minute."

"They make us all mad," Derek said.

"They think they're cute," Paige said as she watched their departure. "What a couple of idiots. They think anything they don't understand is dumb. That's a classic sign of stupidity."

Derek felt his anger subside slightly as he heard her words. He was glad to hear her saying that. She wasn't taken in by typical jock theatrics.

He watched her across the table as she brushed her hair back. She was wearing a long tee shirt and white leggings today, and she looked as beautiful as ever. Derek forgot about everything else. The weekend was a day away, but it would not come soon enough. He wanted the date to begin now.

"Pencil them in on the map," Paige said. "I want them to get in the way of the monsters."

"That can be arranged," Geoff said, imitating a Bela Lugosi accent.

44

"Him and all his friends," Paige added. "Those snob girls and all of them."

After a few minutes the workshop got under way, and a girl named Veronica Mallory got up and read a piece she had prepared from *A Coney Island of the Mind*.

A series of readings followed. The quality was mixed. Some kids stumbled, some got nervous, some spat when they hit words with strong consonants.

Alex's reading of a Langston Hughes poem was a highlight. He had obviously worked hard the night before, because he had a strong delivery. He rarely had to look at the page of the small paperback he held, and he made frequent eye contact.

Derek and the others clapped when he was finished, and when he was seated everyone at the table congratulated him.

"My dad gave me some pointers," he said. "It's one of his favorite poems."

Geoff read a short piece from Thurber before the workshop period ended, but neither Paige nor Derek had time to read their pieces. Derek couldn't complain. He didn't really want to get up in front of the group today, not after the encounter with Joseph.

The next class period would be soon enough.

As the kids began to file out stage left, he and Paige walked together, and she confessed relief as well.

Geoff and Alex were waiting. "Shall we play?" Geoff asked. "If we get started, we could kind of figure out how it works, make up some rules."

"We'll need sort of a controller, won't we?" Paige asked. "Like a dungeon master in D&D?"

"Yeah, somebody will have to do that," Geoff agreed.

"You'd be the logical choice," Derek said. "You did the map and all."

"Yeah, but I want to play. I mean, you know, I want to use my monster and all."

"You do it, Derek," Paige suggested.

He shook his head. "Not me. I'm not organized enough. What about you, Paige?"

"I don't know enough about monsters," she said. They all looked at Alex.

He smiled, thought it over a minute, and then threw up his hands. "Why not?" He gave an insidious laugh.

"Uh-oh, the power's going to his head," Paige joked.

Alex continued his laugh, bringing one hand up to his face, miming a cape. "Won't you all join me?"

Since Derek's mom was at work, they decided his living room would give them the best place to play. They wouldn't be disturbed, so they all agreed to meet around one P.M. That gave everyone a chance to dash home for lunch.

Derek heated some of the leftover Chinese food in the microwave and had just finished it when Paige arrived. Geoff wasn't far behind, and Alex showed up only a few minutes after that.

"I guess we're ready to play," Derek said.

They cleared the coffee table in the living room and spent a few minutes devising a method of scoring strikes against each other, and then the game was off. Since they hadn't really established a set of rules, they agreed the first session would be a test run with everyone contributing.

As things progressed, it became clear the activity would be a blend of storytelling and competition. Since Alex was the controller for this round, he set the stage by describing their nightmare world, the neighborhoods, the streets, and the Nightmare Wood.

It was more than the wood they'd made their way through the day before, however. In his version it was a much eerier place, a place visited at night, shrouded in shadow and mist. The latter made Paige happy, since it would mean her monster could conceal itself easily.

Alex pointed out that the darkness would conceal the other monsters as well, and he allowed each player to select a hiding place from the map, positions they informed him of with a whisper in order to keep the location secret from the others.

Once that was decided, Alex took a few moments to decide on some variable to keep the game interesting, making some notes to himself.

"I guess we're ready to play," he said.

"Let's do the candles again," Paige injected. "That made it more eerie."

Derek looked over at the window. With the curtains closed, it would shut out the sun, and his mom had some utility candles she kept in case of power outages.

He found them in a drawer in the kitchen along with a box of matches. After he'd closed the curtains, he lit the candles and placed them in holders.

The room suddenly seemed like a different place with an eerie gold glow from the flames illuminating the table and casting shadows across everyone's faces.

"Does seem more appropriate," Geoff mused. "Let's play."

"It's midnight," Alex began. "Monsters come out at midnight." He grinned as he let that thought sink in.

"The night is still; each of you is in your chosen position. You look around, then you decide what you want to do."

"What's our objective?" Derek asked. "We need an object for the game."

"You want to be king of the Nightmare Wood," Alex said. "You want to fight off the other monsters and claim the woods as your lair."

"That works, but we need something more," Paige said. "We have to try to figure out where each other are hiding, and along the way ..." She hesitated a moment, and in the glow of the candlelight her face seemed almost maniacal as she smiled. "We collect as many victims as possible. We are monsters, after all."

"Monsters can't be played the same way heroes are," Geoff agreed.

"I thought we were more like sympathetic monsters," Derek said. "You know, like Frankenstein."

"Frankenstein's monster," Alex corrected. "The monster didn't have a name."

"Whatever," Derek said. "You understand what I'm saying."

"We're playing monsters, we should make them as much like monsters as possible," Geoff said. "Let's make it a complete experience, something we can really get into. Humans are the enemy."

"That's kind of a dark mood," Derek said.

"Come on," Alex protested. "Afraid you can't handle thinking like a monster? It's for fun. I promise I won't let it turn you into a serial killer when you grow up."

With a shrug Derek conceded. If they were going to play it that way, he could make his monster as dangerous as any of them.

Quickly they made note of their positions on some paper from Derek's pad. Then they prepared to keep track of their movements on the paper, fashioning their own version of the map spread before them. They each were developing personal game kits, it seemed.

"You've got to use your imagination," Alex said. "We'll have monster confrontations, and each game will be ongoing until someone wins. Then we'll start over, and we'll score the number of times a person wins. Remember, I've got obstacles on my map, and there may be other monsters, too. If you're going to be preying on victims, you're bound to aggravate local law enforcement."

"What determines a game?" Paige asked.

"Last monster standing," Alex said.

A right-to-left rotation was agreed upon, so Geoff began.

"My creature, the Feline, sniffs the air," he said. "And its whiskers perk, seeking sensations."

"The night is chilly. You don't smell much besides the forest where you are now," Alex said.

"The Feline moves forward," Geoff said. "Eight paces."

Derek could imagine the quick, catlike creature, its eyes glowing green in the darkness as it progressed through the underbrush, feet padding softly on the forest floor even though it was swift.

"Some mist is rising from the ground there," Alex said. "Now you do sniff something, something that's not what you're used to. It's not mist at all." .

"Is it Paige's monster?" Geoff asked.

"You don't know that. It's something the Feline has never smelled before," Alex pointed out.

"I, I mean, the Feline looks around."

"About four paces to the right, the Feline sees the outline of something, but it can't quite make out what it is," Alex said.

"You looked at my monster, you know it has strong night vision," Geoff said.

"Yeah, but he can't see what's up there. He's got to get closer if that's what he wants."

"Okay," Geoff said. "He moves."

"And he walks right through this cloud of mist that doesn't part when he moves. It swirls around him, covering him, dragging him toward the ground."

"It's me!" Paige said with a sinister smile. "My monster."

Geoff slammed his hand down on the table so hard he almost knocked over the candles. "It's time for a fight," he said.

And with Alex monitoring the conflict, the first round of the club's first battle of the Nightmare Wood continued.

Derek found himself gripping the arms of his chair.

The excitement made him tense as he waited for a turn, but he also had a mysterious feeling that something was not right, that something very weird was happening. He felt as if his energy was being drained as things proceeded.

The voices of the others sounded far away, and the events he was imagining were becoming more real, as if he were watching them in a film rather than just thinking them up.

Maybe it was even more real than that—more like he was taking on an ethereal form and hovering over the events, not watching a film but looking at a reality.

Everything else was in slow motion—everything that Alex, Geoff, and Paige did. He started to mention what he was feeling, but he held his words. He didn't want to seem crazy.

He had to remind himself once again it was just a game, a game, a game. He wished he could believe that as his turn came around.

"Okay, it's dark and Ogre is on the prowl," he said. "He's outside the wood, heading along Johnson Street. What does he see?"

Alex consulted his notes. "There's a guy there, walking home late. He's in a hurry, but he has an eerie sensation that something's following him."

"He needs an eerie sensation that something's going to get him," Derek warned.

Joseph Stanley was hoofing it because his Firebird was in the shop. He'd rounded a curve with a little too much speed, and he'd scraped the paint off one side.

Being without transportation wouldn't have been a problem, except Sandi, who would otherwise have given him a ride, had decided to go shopping.

He hadn't wanted to spend the afternoon watching her try on dresses, so he was on his own. It was a hot day for it, too. He decided to cut through Johnson Street to his neighborhood as a short cut.

He was about halfway along the street when the sound of the wind picked up. At first he welcomed the breeze, but after moving a few steps, he realized the wind was unusually cold.

It was too cold for a summer wind, almost as cold as a wind from late December. He folded his arms and turned around, trying to see where it was coming from.

There was nothing there, nothing at all. But he thought he saw something, just a flutter of movement. Maybe he was mistaken, but he thought he'd seen someone duck between two buildings.

He had to be wrong. Nobody would be following him. People knew better than to mess with him, and if the geeks tried making fun of him again, he'd show them. They'd be sorry, really sorry.

He didn't bother to walk back and check to see if anyone was hiding. He had better things to do.

Spinning around, he continued to walk in the direction he had been heading. He'd have his car back in another day, and he wouldn't walk then. He'd fly. He liked to get out on the roads outside town and take the car to the max. His old man covered the gas and the scrapes, and what was the point of having a hot car if you didn't make the most of it?

He'd traveled another few feet when another wind blast hit him, and in the same instant, he heard heavy footfalls on the pavement. He didn't hear the clack of shoe soles, however, so he speculated that a dog might be approaching. It'd have to be a big one, maybe the Great Dane that lived on Collins Drive.

Even if that mutt wanted to be friendly he'd have problems. He glanced back over his shoulder, or at least started to. Before he completed the movement, something shot forward, clipping him on the side of his skull.

The force of the blow jolted his head, and huge black dots formed in front of his eyes. The dots seemed to grow larger and larger, threatening to blot out his vision completely.

He had to shake his head to keep from fainting, and as he staggered, reaching out for some kind of support, something else hit him.

It felt like a punch, though it was more like a hard shove at the center of his back. He was pitched forward into a cluster of trash cans that had been set out for the sanitation department.

As he plowed into them, the cans toppled, spilling their putrid contents everywhere. The stench of rotting food and other refuse filled his nostrils as he tried to pick himself up.

His head was still spinning, and he couldn't figure out what had happened. If there was a dog after him, it moved like lightning.

On his hands and knees, he crawled out of the garbage, and managed to get back to his feet with a little effort. Then he shook his head again, trying to clear his brain and vision.

The move didn't work. His vision remained blurred. Cautiously, he tried to look around and get a look at whatever had attacked him. Could even a big dog have hit so hard?

He heard the breathing somewhere to his right and turned in that direction. Blinking, he tried to get a clear view of the figure standing there, but he couldn't focus. All he could see was some massive mass of fur.

The animal seemed to be crouching near the mouth of the alley, a large gray tangle of fur. He wondered if it might be a sheepdog or some other breed.

It was unquestionably a large breed. He took a step back. They said you were supposed to walk backward to escape a dog. He moved slowly, one step back, then the other.

As he moved, he heard a low growl. There was nothing wrong with his hearing, and the sound was terrifying. It was a warning sound, a threatening sound.

Awkwardly, he bent his knees, lowering himself to the sidewalk. With one hand, he felt around until he could find a garbage can lid. Then he straightened again. The animal was still crouched in the same spot.

Was it watching him? He couldn't tell. He couldn't make out its features or the shape of its head.

That didn't matter. All he needed was a general idea of where it was. Raising the lid, he hurled it like a discus toward the animal.

He expected the flying implement to frighten the beast away, but even with his clouded vision, he saw an appendage extend and knock the lid aside.

That almost made Joseph's heart stop. How could a dog do that? Without thinking further about rational action, he turned, letting panic take command.

He ran, stumbling over garbage in his path but kicking free of it before he toppled to the ground. He could hear the thing, whatever it was, moving behind him, running after him, its feet padding against the ground.

He knew he couldn't afford to let it catch him. Pumping his legs hard, he rushed as fast as he could. He raised one hand in front of him since he couldn't see well, holding it forward to deflect anything that might be in front of him.

He couldn't remember being this frightened in a long time, not since he'd believed in the bogey man, because whatever was behind him reminded him of the bogey man. It was something he'd never seen before.

As he neared the corner of the street, he felt something snatching at his shirt, and he realized the fabric was tearing.

He realized that he shouldn't have hoped to outrun the creature, not if it could move as fast as it had in attacking him. It was going to rip him to shreds. He tried to prepare himself for the pain even as he rushed around a corner and almost plowed into a guy on a bicycle.

The bike whooshed past, and he jerked back to avoid a collision.

"What's with you?" the bike rider asked.

"I was trying to … trying to …"

He turned and realized that whatever he'd been trying to outrun was no longer around. He blinked, and while his vision was still fuzzy, he could tell the dog or whatever it had been was not there any longer. "You seeing things?" the biker asked.

"I don't know. I thought this dog was after me."

"Guess again, dude."

As the biker pedaled away, he leaned against the wall. Had he stumbled and hit his head and imagined everything else?

No way.

Something had been after him. Something had hit him. Something had...he reached back with difficulty to touch his shirt. Something had torn his shirt. Something with sharp claws.

Something that had wanted to eat him alive.

Chapter Eight

Felines or Tygers or Ogres?

First dates can be terrifying.

Derek realized that as he dressed in a fresh pair of jeans and a crisply laundered Oxford shirt his mother had helped him iron. For a while, the prospect of a new girl took his mom's mind off Neil, and she helped him get ready. She was amused by Derek's excitement, but the preparations seemed to draw them close again.

When it was time to leave, he drew a couple of deep breaths to calm himself and then started the drive to Paige's. He managed to make it to her door without fainting or running the car in the ditch, but he had to keep telling himself to relax.

Before Paige appeared he had to answer a few of her dad's questions, an experience that was unnerving but nothing he couldn't handle.

He felt himself almost teetering when she entered, wearing a short denim skirt and a blue tee shirt. Her hair was brushed out and fell in curls to her shoulders. With her dark brown eyes and dimples, she almost seemed to be a dream.

"Are you ready?" he asked after blinking to keep from staring.

"I guess so." He hoped he'd be able to steer.

The theater, a historic old building, was in the downtown area, although the mall also had a multiplex. He liked to go to the old theater which featured ornate designs and rich red curtains. It was the way a movie ought to be viewed.

This movie proved to be a blast with plenty of laughs even though it had a serious theme. That made Derek feel a little more relaxed. He'd worried the picture might be a dog, with him guilty by association, but with both of them laughing, that set an upbeat tone for the evening.

The rain started about midway through the film. Even over the theater's sound system, the storm became audible, pelting rain on the roof. It subsided some time before the show was over, but when Derek and Paige were ready to leave, the dampness was still heavy in the air.

The summer heat used the rain to form a sauna, in fact, so that as they moved down the theater steps, they could see mist rising from the sidewalk.

Darkness had come by that time, and the street-lamps were on, glistening off the puddles and the sheen of rain left on the streets. The light also illuminated the mist, making the wisps look ghostlike.

"This is almost spooky," Paige said as they decided to walk for a while through the downtown area.

"Sort of," Derek agreed. He squeezed her hand, which he was holding again, and that seemed to prompt her to draw closer to him. He wasn't that frightened even with his active imagination, and he couldn't complain about the eeriness if getting Paige closer was the result.

As they edged out of the shop area and started moving along the quieter residential streets, he felt a little of his confidence ebb, however.

There were almost no cars here, and all the people seemed to be locked away in their houses, safe behind walls that would insulate them from outside sounds, such as screams for help.

Derek hoped they wouldn't have to utter any.

He tried to concentrate on the warmth of Paige's hand in his and the occasional brush of her shoulder. That was wonderful.

He was reminded of a scene from *The Wizard of Oz* as they continued their walk, the one where the characters huddled together, rolled their eyes and watched for "lions and tigers and bears, oh my." Paige and he began to look around, checking trees and shadows for signs of movement, or monsters.

"I almost wish we hadn't played 'Terror Club' so much all week," Paige confessed. "I feel like we're walking through the game."

"It is just a game," Derek reminded her. He almost believed it.

"Yeah, I know, but right now I almost think it could be real."

She nodded toward the corner where a cloud of mist was swirling in the pool of light from a street-lamp. "That could be Vapor," she said.

They stopped as they considered that possibility. It almost seemed comical, but after a moment of hesitating, they crossed the street, avoiding the light.

Derek began to check over his shoulder also, just making sure neither Ogre nor the Feline, nor, for that matter, Tyger, were anywhere in sight.

"Let's not be goofy," he said. "There are no monsters."

"We both know that," Paige said. "Except it's dark."

They stopped for a moment, looked around, smiled at each other, and in an instant, a split instant, they kissed.

Her lips were soft and warm, and Derek suddenly felt so lightheaded it was as if he'd been lifted off his feet. As he pulled back, he wasn't sure what to say.

"I'm glad you asked me out," Paige said, breaking the awkwardness.

"I'm glad you agreed."

They began to walk again, arm in arm now, her head on his shoulder. As a light breeze pushed back some of the humidity and the mist, he almost felt like whistling, until they heard the cries of pain.

The sound seemed to hang on the breeze, a high, shrill screech.

"What is that?" Paige asked as once again they stopped in their tracks.

"I'm not sure," Derek said as he looked around in the darkness, trying to figure out which direction the sound was coming from. He wasn't even sure if it was human, but he knew it was chilling.

"We've got to try to help!" Paige said.

He agreed, but he had to admire her for the impulse. That helped him muster his own courage, and they began to run along the sidewalk.

Finally they decided the cries were coming from a point ahead of them and to the left. It was a small lot in a curve, and no houses had been built there. There were only trees and untended grass which grew thick and tall.

"Could it be a baby?" Paige asked breathlessly as they jogged forward, covering the two hundred feet between them and the shadowy ground.

"I don't know," Derek said again.

As they reached the lot, they jumped off the sidewalk and began making their way through the grass, knocking the tall leaves aside and dodging trees and low-hanging branches.

"This is almost as bad as the woods," Paige said.

Derek agreed as they plunged deeper into the shadows. With the trees, the light from the street-lamps was shaded back. The noises grew more intense as they continued. Derek fought an impulse to turn back, and shoved more branches aside.

"Something's moving up there!" Paige shouted, pointing forward.

He did see something stirring, or at least he saw branches moving. It could've been the wind, but he didn't think so.

"Maybe an animal's caught in a trap or something," Paige suggested.

Or maybe there's a monster, he thought.

They pushed on, and he thought he could make out the outline of something large in the shadows, and he thought he heard something grunting.

In a heartbeat, he realized the chilling screams had quieted.

"What is it?" Paige asked, her voice almost a scream.

That made the grunting stop, and then some branches and brush up ahead rattled, as if something were retreating.

He and Paige continued moving, though they'd slowed their pace. They crept ahead, bending slightly, placing their footsteps carefully.

"What do you think it was?" Paige asked. Her hand was on his arm now, her fingers tightening.

"An animal of some kind," Derek said. He had other ideas as well, but he saw no need to alarm her. It couldn't be any of the things he was thinking about. Could it?

"This lot is deeper than it looked," Paige said. "It's long," he said. "An edge lot."

They moved around the thick trunk of a tree and spotted the remains.

"A dog," Paige said. "A poor little dog."

The animal had been mauled, and what was left wasn't moving. Derek put his arms around Paige as she placed her face against his shoulder.

"How awful," she said. "Poor little thing."

"Something really tore it up," Derek said.

"What could it have been?"

"Maybe a bigger dog, or some other kind of animal," he speculated.

But he was really thinking—something like Felines or Tygers or Ogres!

Chapter Nine

Mail Call

They'd been playing the game about a week and a half when the packets arrived. By then, most of the problems and rules had been ironed out, so they were becoming immersed in the experience.

Derek's house had become the game site of choice, since his mom was usually at work, and they could play undisturbed. Geoff explained that his mom still wasn't ready for visitors.

Alex remained the controller with a promise that he'd be able to cycle into the game at a later point and let someone else take over the larger duties. Benefits of a change seemed to be twofold. First, it would give Alex a chance to play, and it would give the game a chance to start fresh, thus keeping the play interesting.

Geoff was designated as the replacement, and no one doubted he'd do a good job. He almost seemed to be looking forward to it, in fact, even though he remained wild about being a player.

Maybe wild wasn't the word. He played as if his life depended on it, as if the game was all that mattered in his life.

Despite that devotion, he wasn't a constant winner. Derek and Paige had held their own with several wins to each of their monsters' credits, claiming victims, battling angry mobs of townspeople and taking on each other.

Vapor was a hard monster to spot, but Derek's Ogre had cunning which also made him formidable, while the quickness and wiliness of the Feline sometimes allowed Geoff the upper hand.

Alex was good at taking all factors into account, and that kept things exciting. The routine of heading for a game after the workshop developed, and the suspense between games was almost unbearable. They all looked forward to getting back to the hunt.

Derek realized that with the fun the game provided and the burgeoning relationship with Paige, the summer was shaping up better than he ever could've expected. That was in spite of the snobs who were constantly reminding them in one way or another of their presence.

He and Paige had put the trauma of finding the dog behind them. Paige had remained upset the day after their date, and he had felt edgy as well. Reading assignments helped distract them. At first he thought Paige might not want to play the game anymore after seeing actual violence, but they talked it over and decided their monsters were just for fun. They didn't have anything to do with real-life tragedies.

It was after a morning class in which Paige had read British poetry that he and Paige found the first packet. It had been a particularly difficult class because as Paige read, the snobs had played a subtle game, trying to break her concentration.

As Paige had started to read, Amber had started coughing, keeping it up just long enough to be annoying before pretending to get her throat clear.

Paige didn't let it fluster her, but after she'd finished her first poem, Denise Hubbard accidentally, on purpose, edged a stack of paperbacks off the table in front of her. The sound was not loud, since the books had soft covers, but as they splatted to the floor Paige hesitated.

She didn't let it rattle her for long, however. She continued reading, concentrating on her presentation and making her voice heard.

Derek looked over at Ms. Stone, who was seeing all the activity, but she couldn't really take action. The snobs would only proclaim the innocence of their actions.

When Suzi began to giggle, Derek thought he was going to explode with anger. Why couldn't they just let Paige read? Why did they have to continue harassing her?

As Suzi giggled, seemingly at nothing, the laughter became infectious. Denise began to laugh and then kids at other tables began to laugh at her uncontrollable laughter.

Paige tried to keep going, but the giggling got so bad that Ms. Stone had to get up and admonish the students to settle down.

"Let's act like young adults," she warned.

"Sorry," Suzi said. "I thought of something funny I saw on a show."

Paige finished hurriedly, just wanting to sit down. Being in front of a group was hard for anyone. Having added tension made it awful. She was fighting tears as she settled into her seat next to Derek.

"I shouldn't let them get to me," she said. "That was nothing."

Alex patted her arm softly. "It's okay. Just ignore them."

"Yeah," Derek agreed. "They're acting like fifth graders."

Paige nodded and touched a finger to her eye to stop a tear. "It's okay. It's over."

Paige and Derek splurged on hamburgers again since his mom had just given him his allowance. It was supposed to take their minds off the snobs.

They almost enjoyed the meal even though Jude Sheffield and Denise were in the next booth. Denise, dressed in a designer outfit that was worth about the same amount as Derek's car, had spent most of the meal talking loudly to Jude about a modeling assignment she had.

She obviously wanted Paige to hear her, but Derek and Paige made a point of talking and laughing loudly themselves, just to goad the other couple.

"What is it with those people?" Paige asked when they were back in the car.

"I don't know what to make of them," Derek said. "There's just no excuse for them. They're bored and we happen to be the way they've picked to liven things up for themselves."

He drove back to his house to pick up his game materials, and they decided to talk about something else.

As he pulled into the driveway, he stopped to check the mailbox and as usual found most items were for his mom. Only a brown envelope at the bottom of the stack had an address label with his name on it.

"What's that?" Paige asked.

"I'm not sure," he said. Quickly he slipped his finger under the flap and ripped it open.

There were several pieces of paper inside. As the motor idled, he began to shuffle through the materials. He found a typed cover letter first, and he was excited when he recognized the Scare logo at the top. "It must be about the contest," he said.

"Dear Mr. Cliver," the letter began. "We appreciate your participation in our Terror Club campaign. We were happy to receive your letter about your monster."

"What does it say?" Paige asked.

"It's about the Terror Club," he said, reading on aloud so that she didn't have to just stand there. "We received many interesting entries, and we're still looking over them. We are enclosing materials for a Terror Club game for your interest while you await contest results."

"That must be what some of the rest of this stuff is," Paige said, taking other items from his hands.

"Probably stuff we've already done ourselves," Derek said.

"Well let's see," Paige said. "I think we have ..."

"... a set of runes," Alex said later that afternoon as they looked over the package that had arrived in his family's mail.

"I've heard of runes," Derek said. "But I'm not sure exactly what they are."

"My dad was a Tolkien fan in college, so all of the kids had read *The Hobbit* by the time we finished sixth grade," Alex said. "That's where I read about them. They're ancient writings."

They were all sitting around a card table in his family's den looking over the parchment-like paper that had been included in each package. The writings were different on each, but there was no real explanation for what the lettering meant.

"Maybe this is supposed to be the name for our monsters. It's obviously just enclosed because it looks like it's magical," Alex suggested.

"Probably so," Derek agreed.

"So what about this other stuff?" Paige asked. "The paper for the making of a map I can understand, but what about these..."

"...game tiles," Geoff said. He was holding a couple of the small cardboard squares that had been included in his packet. They had frightening monster faces on them, faces something like the stone gargoyles and matched the tiles in each of the other packets.

Paige had seen the gargoyles before in cultural travel books her mother owned. She described the old photographs as they gathered in her living room in late afternoon for a game. "I think they were water spouts or something," she said.

"These tiles must be meant to mark your monster's position," Geoff said. "They just wanted to give a generic monster look to them. Our monsters are better."

"Really," Derek agreed. He looked over his own tiles. They were different enough to distinguish them from those in other packets, yet obviously similar. "I hope if they draw our actual monsters for the magazine that they do a better job."

Paige picked up her markers from the packet her father had brought home from their post office box. "Yeah, they're just basic. I guess they'll do, though. The runes and the map paper will at least spruce the game up.

"That's true," Alex said. "It's more like we're playing an official game this way, rather than something we just came up with."

"I think we still did a good job," Geoff said.

"Yeah, we did," Alex agreed.

The game was proving addictive. They usually played until parents interrupted for supper or chores, and then they couldn't wait until the next day for another round.

"Well, are we going to use the stuff for this round?" Geoff asked.

"Might as well," Alex said. "Of course we can't really place the tiles on the board until a location of a monster is known, but the graphs for the map should come in handy."

"And the runes will be the official designations for our monsters," Derek said.

"Yeah. We won't be able to pronounce it, but we'll know."

And once again they began, their imaginations transforming the living room into a spooky place of shadows and mist.

Derek imagined himself in Ogre's place, moving menacingly through the forest, his sharp eyes rolling left and right, scanning the landscape, ever cautious. There were other monsters and dangers as well.

Alex had introduced obstacles, such as traps set by townspeople who'd discovered there were monsters nearby. The players' monsters had to be wary also of others in the environment. Alex had introduced sheriff's patrols, and of course there were victims.

"You see a girl walking along the street," Alex said as Paige took her turn with Vapor. "She's in a hurry but she's all alone."

"Vapor's hungry," Paige said.

"The girl looks around," Alex said, letting his voice drop to a whisper. "She senses something. There are tingling sensations of fear on the back of her neck. She checks over her shoulder, but there's nothing but … mist."

"Vapor starts to swirl," Paige said. "She's moving. Getting closer. The girl is Denise Hubbard, right?" She chuckled at the thought. "She's coming back from a modeling assignment."

"You can't do the description," Geoff protested. "Alex has to do that."

"I'm just joking," Paige said. "Denise tried to spoil lunch for us today. Sometimes I wish she'd get in Vapor's way."

"Sometimes I agree with you," Alex said.

They all laughed at the thought.

"Like we could really work magic with the game," Paige said. "Not in a million years, but if we could…"

Derek suddenly felt uncomfortable. This round seemed even more intense than usual, requiring a great deal of energy. A drowsy feeling crept over him, and his fingers grew numb.

His brain felt as if a mist had settled over it, and the room around him became less defined while the scenes in his imagination became more real, more specific.

When his turn came, he found he was submerged in the monster world. He could imagine the rasp of Ogre's breath and the rustle of leaves as he moved. He could picture Ogre's feet, settling hard on the forest floor, and he could even visualize the look on his creature's face. There was a slight scowl, and his nose twitched, seeking odors that might alert him to further danger or offer further advantage against his opponents.

It was almost too real. Derek could hear Alex's voice, talking him through the steps, but it seemed distant, almost like the echo of an echo.

As Vapor's pursuit of her victim continued, he found that seeming real also, with Paige's descriptions of the chase almost played like a film he was watching. The victim ran, terrified, uncertain of what was chasing her.

It was like being in a trance. It didn't seem like he was playing a game anymore. It seemed like he was there.

The darkness seemed real, as did the sounds of night. He progressed slowly through the trees and branches, inching forward, watching for others.

Derek realized he almost seemed to be inside Ogre, looking out through his keen eyes, the night vision already adjusted and making it possible for him to see into shadows that might otherwise have been impenetrable.

"What's going on?" he asked himself, but the question did not leave his lips. He was paying attention only to the night and only to the forest.

Branches parted for his bulk, but then something rustled. Before he knew it, he was looking into the glaring eyes of the Feline. He wanted to kick himself. He should've known to be looking upward, but he had failed to do so, and the catlike creature had pounced, landing in a crouched position in front of him, ready to strike.

The gleaming green eyes with the vertical pupils peered at him, and the fangs, like curved needles, were bared and ready.

Ogre's feet were planted wide to steady his massive body, and then, the cat-creature pounced, front claws thudding into his chest. The blow didn't manage to knock him off balance, but a roar of pain escaped his lips as the claws dug through the furry coat and into flesh.

They raked down his torso, drawing blood.

Clenching massive hands into fists, Ogre slammed simultaneous blows into the Feline's ribs. The blows were enough to stun but not enough to drive the creature back.

Ogre was preparing for another blow, when Derek was rattled back to reality. He wasn't Ogre, he wasn't in Ogre's brain.

He was here, in the real world, sitting at a real table with real friends. He looked around at the faces of the other players.

Alex was staring at him, one eyebrow cocked up quizzically.

"Guess I got a little too into it," Derek said, wiping a touch of perspiration from his brow.

Paige massaged her eyes with a delicate touch of her fingertips. "Maybe we all did."

"I was beginning to wonder if all of you were thinking this was real," Alex said. "Be cool, folks."

"It's fun," Geoff said. "Don't knock it."

"It's fun, but it's just a game," Paige reminded. "A game that's given me a headache. Gosh, maybe I've been concentrating too hard. Hope I haven't been wishing too hard that things are real."

Derek laughed. "Maybe we're all just concentrating too hard."

He reached for his game packet, and as he picked it up, the rune fluttered out and drifted down to the table. As it rested there, a distinct green glow seemed to emanate from the letters.

"Look at that," Paige said.

"I see it," Derek whispered. "Weird."

Paige pulled her rune out quickly. The same glow seemed to be coming from her letters.

"What is it?" Alex asked.

"They're glowing," Paige said.

"It's probably just the light or something," Geoff said. "It'd be neat if it were real, wouldn't it?"

"If it were real, yeah," Alex said. "I think we're all concentrating too hard now."

When Alex held up his rune, there was no glow, and as Derek looked back at his, the glow seemed to be gone.

But he hadn't imagined that, had he? There had been a glow, a distinct green aura.

Chapter Ten

Water Torture

Denise's modeling assignment was for a local department store planning a summer swimwear sale. The advertising agent was a friend of her father's and had pulled some strings to get her the job.

Doing pictures that would appear in a local newspaper supplement and some other print ads didn't really excite her, but she had heard one of the best photographers in Pembrook would be doing the shoot. She had wanted the job mainly because she wanted the photos for her portfolio.

She needed new pictures to get into any of the really good teen magazines. They would be a springboard into other publications, and hopefully by the time she graduated she'd be able to look to a career.

As the photographer and his assistant set up cameras and lights beside the inside pool at the Pembrook Health and Racquet Club, she slipped off the robe she wore over the black suit they'd given her, a nice one that looked great on her. She had decided that in the dressing room. She was hoping they'd let her keep it.

While she waited on them to call her, she adjusted the suit slightly, then ran her hands through her hair, letting locks slide slowly through her fingers. She always liked the way that felt, and she wanted it to look a little wild in the pictures. That would help her appear exotic.

"Okay, Denise," the photographer called. He was only about twenty, and he was good looking with curly black hair.

She wondered if he'd be interested in a high-school girl. She had Jude, but a guy like Hatter McDonald could be important for her.

She took her place at poolside and struck a quick pose as he instructed her. As the camera began to whir, she let her eyes close just slightly, trying for seductive.

"Okay, good," Hatter said. "That's great. Keep moving for me."

She obliged, raising her arms, bending her legs, turning her head, tossing her hair about. She smiled, acted surprised, wet her lips with her tongue, and made other expressions all in quick succession.

"You're beautiful," Hatter said. "This is great, but hang on a second."

He looked over his shoulder to the short dark-haired girl who'd come with him.

"We seem to be getting some steam off the pool," he said. "Would you check with the guys up there and see if they've got the heater on or something?"

"Sure."

The girl left, and they continued. The camera motor continued to whir, and Denise continued to strike poses. She felt fabulous. She knew she was beautiful. She'd been told that since she'd been a child, but this confirmed it. She was going to be on magazine covers. She might even get film deals. Or her own exercise video!

"Step a little closer," Hatter said. "I'm still getting vapor off the pool. I don't know what the hell it is, but if they don't shut it down, it's going to look like you're in a fog."

Denise just kept looking at the camera, smiling, laughing.

She didn't notice that the mist that had formed across the surface of the pool was beginning to move and swirl, crawling across the still water.

Since she filled Hatter's frame, he didn't notice either. He was busy speaking encouragement and suggestions.

"Okay, lift your hair. Beautiful. You're doing great."

Denise laughed as they continued. She was still thrilled even though she had to keep smiling and moving. They always said models worked hard.

She looked forward into Hatter's camera, not back. She didn't pay any attention to the pool or the mist, which was now rising, reaching up from the edge of the pool, climbing higher and higher.

When it began to swirl around her she was confused. They were supposed to be taking care of the problem, but it seemed to be getting worse.

She did turn now and discovered a wall of smoke was there. The sight frightened her, and the fear seemed to build, churning her insides. It turned quickly into terror. She found herself so frightened, so consumed by this intense fear, that she couldn't speak.

"This is ridiculous. We'll have to get a fan to clear this," Hatter said, but his voice was far away.

She was lost in the mist, and as she tried to walk out of it, she couldn't find her way. She was being smothered. She was trapped inside this cloud, and it was beginning to spin around her body, climbing up to her throat. It was a small tornado of mist.

The grip on her throat seemed almost like hands. She tried to breathe but couldn't, and the scream that formed in her throat could not escape her lips.

Her eyes rolled back in her head, and she felt herself spinning downward, down and down into darkness.

Chapter Eleven

The Hour of Nightmares

"Okay, you got her," Derek said, looking at the game map spread on the table. A marker had been placed to indicate the site where Vapor had finally captured her victim.

"It was a tough chase, though," Paige said, wiping her brow. She'd spent each of her turns at the game continuing the pursuit of Vapor's victim. "Good thing it was just a game. I was so mad at Denise and all of the snobs, it was like I was really after her." She began to laugh. "Like our game could generate magic or whatever."

"If it worked, we could just take care of all the snobs," Derek said.

"Dream on," Alex said. "We're just going to have to learn to live with them."

Chuckling, they finished gathering their materials and thanked Mrs. Laningham on their way out. Paige followed them to the front door.

"I'll call you in a while," she told Derek as he headed outside.

He smiled back, then waved to Alex and Geoff as they headed off. He climbed into his car.

"We can play at my house tomorrow," Alex called before the car door closed. "My dad won't mind us using his den."

Derek nodded his agreement. The remark made him think of his own father and his absence, even though he was in no hurry to sign Neil on for the job.

As he drove up his street, he thought about the depth the game had developed. It was almost disconcerting to consider. He'd heard about kids who'd become too deeply involved in role-playing games. There had even been television shows about it.

He didn't want to let himself get sucked into it so far that he couldn't think rationally anymore. It was for fun. It wasn't his whole life.

Pulling to a stop when he reached his driveway, he shut off the Mustang's engine. He headed inside, deciding he wouldn't think any more about the Terror Club for the rest of the afternoon.

After all, with any luck Paige would call soon.

He only had to wait a half hour before the phone rang.

"What's going on?" Paige asked when he picked up the handset.

"Just bumming around."

"The game got deep today, didn't it?"

"Yeah, I know," Derek agreed.

"I guess I was just so mad at all the snobs I really got into it."

"That's what it's for, escapism," Derek said. "We just have to remember not to take it too seriously."

"We probably need to do something besides the game."

"Yeah, I think we are spending a lot of time hovering over our maps."

"That's true. I thought we could do something outside this afternoon, maybe go swimming," Paige said. "You want to?"

"Sure. Sounds like fun."

"I heard there was a place near here, a lake or whatever."

"Yeah. It's not far."

"You want to go there? We could bike over in about a half hour?"

"I'll meet you at your house," he said.

He changed into cutoffs and an old tee, then waited awhile so he wouldn't arrive on her doorstep too early. After watching minutes tick slowly past he went out, mounted his bike, which he hadn't ridden much lately, and pedaled over to Paige's.

She met him at the door wearing her own cut-offs and tee shirt over her suit. He saw her bike leaning against an oak at the edge of the yard.

"Ready?" she asked.

"Sure."

They climbed aboard and pedaled the short distance. The lake was publicly accessible, but today there were no people around. A lake up the highway with a larger beach area drew the crowds.

Parking their bikes, they draped their towels over a nearby tree branch and began getting ready to swim. Derek kicked off his shoes and almost froze as Paige shrugged off her tee shirt and cutoffs. She was wearing a one-piece with a bright red and blue design, and her long slender legs were tan and firm.

"Hey," she said, wading into the water. "Come on in."

He wasted no time in following. When he reached her, they ran splashing into the water together and swam in a semi-race when the water was deep enough.

The water was warm across the surface from the sun, but as they took turns swimming downward, it proved to be a little colder. Shivering, they climbed out and sat under the oak for a while and began to talk.

As the conversation continued, Derek cautiously edged his hand over and took Paige's. Kissing her before had been fabulous, and he'd been waiting for another opportunity. Now with the water dripping off her hair, she looked fantastic.

Their gazes locked for a second. Then she leaned forward and met his lips.

"I don't know if I'm ready for a boyfriend," she said. "I mean, I'm not sure what I want. You know the story, but I like you."

Derek put an arm around her shoulder. "We'll see what happens," he said.

After talking a while, they dove back into the water and swam some more, then dove under the surface, swimming deeper into the colder water.

Light didn't reach down there as well, and the depths seemed murky, almost frightening. Derek lost sight of Paige after they'd been down a few seconds. Deciding she must've gone to the surface, he headed upward himself. He needed air.

Breaking into the air, he tossed his head back to wipe his eyes. Then as he treaded water, he began to look for Paige.

He couldn't see her anywhere. He looked one way and then another, but all he could find was sunlight glistening off the undisturbed surface of the water. Only his own ripples were visible.

Quickly, he jerked his head toward shore to determine if she'd somehow managed to get there before he had noticed.

Their towels fluttered on the branch where they were hanging, but there was no sign of Paige. "Paige?" he called. "Where are you?"

He didn't get an answer, and anxiety quickly spread through his body. Had something happened to her?

Gulping in a fresh chest full of air, he went under again, swimming downward as quickly as he could, trying to see through the dark water. The bottom was soft and stirred up shimmers of mud which made visibility low.

Frantically he paddled about, trying to search the bottom. What if she had become tangled in the weeds? He held his lips tightly closed even as the pressure in his lungs almost began to ache. He had to find her.

He couldn't let her drown. He fought his way along the bottom, grasping at weeds and other debris, hoping he would locate her.

Having no luck, he finally had to give up and go to the surface. He planned to get a breath and go back down. If she'd been down this long, she would be in trouble.

He couldn't imagine what could've happened in a placid lake, but something must've gone wrong.

He gasped as he broke the surface of the water again. Almost frantic, he began preparing to dive once more. The laughter stopped him.

Paige was beside him, treading water. "You didn't know I could hold my breath so long, did you?" she said, still laughing.

"Very funny," he said, a smile crossing his lips. "You almost scared me to death."

"Oh, did I? Did I really?"

"Well, almost," he said. "For a minute I thought one of the monsters had nabbed you."

"They're not seeming THAT real, are they?" she asked, playfully splashing water toward him.

"Not quite," he said, but as he considered it, he felt a chill. Maybe they were seeming more real than he was willing to admit.

The monsters stalked the night.

The midnight hour chimed, and they emerged, creeping cautiously out of secret places. It was the hour of the hunt, the hour of nightmares.

They looked warily about, then began to stalk, nostrils twitching, seeking some hint of potential victims on the night breeze.

Derek sat at the window that looked out over his front yard. There were no monsters there, but his imagination was alive. He could picture them on the prowl, ready to devour.

No matter how many times he told himself they were only fantasy, he couldn't seem to believe it, not quite. Deep down he sensed something was out there somewhere, something dark and sinister.

Had they somehow created something from their imaginings? It couldn't happen, yet he wondered if somehow they had unleashed some evil that had been waiting for a way to escape upon the world.

"Too many monster movies," he told himself. That was the only explanation.

The phone rang.

The sound exploded into his consciousness, and he almost leapt into the air. Scrambling over to the end table, he answered.

"Were you awake?"

His mom.

"Dozing," he lied.

"Sorry. I just wanted to let you know Neil and I have been delayed."

Derek knew they were attending some kind of party related to Neil's work.

"Neil's boss is taking us out to a late dinner. We won't be really late, but it'll be a while."

"So you're saying don't wait up for you. Don't you have work tomorrow?"

"Yes, but this is important for Neil."

"Sure, Mom. Sure."

"Don't be so hostile. We'll talk later, sweetheart."

"Right."

He placed the handset down again and was about to step away from the phone when it sounded again. The suddenness of the ring again made his muscles tense.

"Hello."

"Derek, were you up?"

This time it was—a pleasant surprise—Paige. "What's up?" he asked.

74

"I am. I couldn't sleep."

"What's wrong?"

"Did you hear the news?"

"No."

"Denise Hubbard was killed."

"What?" He jumped forward in his seat.

"She was modeling swimwear, and she fell beside the pool at the racquet club and hit her head."

He felt the color draining from his face, and a ghostly feeling rattled through him.

"That's weird."

"I know I shouldn't feel guilty, but I was so mad at her," Paige said. "I was even joking about her being Vapor's victim."

"You couldn't have known," he said. "There's no way it could be your fault."

"I wasn't really wishing her dead. She was just so ugly at lunch."

"It's okay," he said softly. "It was an accident."

"It must've happened at the same time we were playing the game. I feel so awful."

"She was mean to you," Derek said. "You had a right to be angry at her. It's awful that she's dead, but it's not your responsibility."

"I know that. I guess I just wanted to hear it from somebody. You don't think .."

"What?"

She hesitated a few seconds. "You don't think the game could've had anything to do with it? I mean, after the dog and all. I'm being stupid. No way. Right?"

"No way," Derek agreed, but he bit his lip after saying it. What if? What if!

"I just keep picturing Vapor sort of floating over the neighborhood, hovering, watching, you know?"

"Stalking?"

"Exactly. It's like she's looking for victims."

Derek swallowed. Did he tell her he had just been experiencing similar feelings of foreboding? That might sound goofy, or it might make her more frightened. She'd called to feel better. On the other hand, if there was a problem, something dangerous, they needed to figure it out.

"I've been kind of thinking the same way," he said. "But it's nothing. Just our imaginations because we've been so intent on playing."

"It can't be real, can it? There aren't really monsters."

"I guess not," he said. "Surely there aren't." But he couldn't be sure. There might be.

There just might be monsters.

Chapter Twelve

Suspicion

A somber mood hung over the crowd when Derek arrived at the workshop the next morning. Many of the kids may not have cared for Denise, but they were still shocked by her death.

At the snob table everyone seemed grim. He was surprised they'd even shown up, but even class must have been better than mourning alone. Only Jude was missing.

Amber's eyes were red-rimmed. She'd probably been crying all night and had come to class only to have somewhere to go. Instead of the usual chatter in the group, everyone was quiet.

Derek's own night had been restless as well. He was feeling almost exhausted. He'd worked some on a piece he was to read, but he felt ill-prepared. He hadn't really been concentrating on it.

None of the kids who took the podium early did very well, but Ms. Stone was supportive, offering suggestions about characterization and inflection. She seemed to be trying to take their minds off the accident by keeping the class moving.

Derek felt there were more important things he needed to think about than a proper reading of the H. G. Wells short story he'd been assigned. It was an interesting piece about a mountain climber who tried to conquer a group of blind people, but he wasn't really focused on it.

When his turn came, as he had hoped it wouldn't, he stammered worse than ever, worse even than the kids who read before him.

He had to stop several times, and only Ms. Stone's constant words of encouragement saw him through it. When he finally finished and closed his book, he bowed his head and ducked back to his seat beside Paige.

She patted his arm, trying to let him know it wasn't that bad.

"I blew it," Derek said.

"You did okay," she whispered back. "Really. No one's really thinking about class."

They listened to a few more readings which finished out the period, and when the period ended they filed out of the gym along with Geoff and Alex.

"Both of you look worn out," Alex observed. He was wearing a black baseball cap which he pushed back on his head. "Is it just the death?"

"We both sort of had dreams about the monsters," Derek said. "Not dreams exactly, but visions, I guess."

One of Alex's eyebrows shot up with surprise. "Maybe we've been at it too hard."

"It's probably nothing," Geoff said.

"Did you have any visions?" Alex asked.

Geoff shook his head. "Not me."

Alex shrugged. "I haven't been playing a monster role, myself. Guess I haven't been into it as deeply as you guys. You think we should tone it back?"

Geoff began to shake his head vigorously, but Derek put his hands into the pockets of the shorts he wore. "I don't know. Paige and I have talked, and we're wondering if something weird is going on. We found a dog killed the other night, then we had these feelings. And Denise died."

"You can't think the game did that," Alex said. "That's just coincidence. The other anxieties are probably because of hearing about the accident."

"I mentioned her while we were playing the game," Paige said. "Could the accident have been caused by my imagination, focused so hard on the game?"

"I don't think so," Alex said.

"Of course not," Geoff said impatiently. His face had turned red. "There's no reason to give the game up. Really! I don't see why you all get so frightened of every little thing. It's silly. We're playing a game, just a game."

The pitch of his voice continued to rise, and his face turned even redder. "I won't give up the game just because one of the blasted snobs had an accident. It's not Paige's fault. It's not our fault!"

Alex reached over and placed a hand on his shoulder to calm him. "Easy, man. We're just considering our options. We're not throwing in the towel."

Geoff exhaled through clenched teeth. His shoulders slumped slightly, and he studied Alex through narrowed eyes. "You sure?"

"Really."

His lips twitched slightly as if he was about to cry. "I'm sorry she got hurt, really. I just don't think it was the game." He looked over at Derek and then at Paige. "I guess I got upset because I don't want to lose the game. You guys are the best friends I've ever had, and I don't want to quit the game."

"We won't quit the game," Derek said. "Don't worry. We're not going to ditch you."

"I know that," Geoff said. "It's just hard not to worry. I've never had friends like you guys. Never."

After class, Derek was planning to walk Paige home, but Ms. Stone caught up with them before they left the parking lot.

"Do you have a minute?" she asked.

Derek hesitated. He wasn't sure what she wanted, and she made him a little nervous. She was wearing a floral print dress today that didn't make her look quite as sinister as her black clothes, but there was still a strangeness about her.

"I'll be okay," Paige said, removing his only excuse to refuse.

"Okay," he said. "What can I do for you?"

"Come on into my office," she said.

Reluctantly, he followed her back into the building and along the narrow hallway that ran behind the stage and past the music department offices.

Her office was a cubbyhole at the end of the hall. The walls were covered with bookshelves lined with drama collections as well as old paperback production copies of plays, and her desk was almost hidden beneath a pile of papers. A couple of framed photographs with Ms. Stone in different costumes from old plays were the only decorations.

She settled into a battered swivel chair and motioned Derek to a seat in a small metal chair.

"You didn't do very well this morning," she said. "I just got a little nervous."

"You've got a lot of potential," she said. "You could be a good actor."

"I could?"

"I don't want to push you into anything you don't want, mind you. This summer is just for fun, but I wondered if anything was bothering you. Anything … extra? Besides Denise."

"Like what?"

"I don't know. I'm not a mind reader."

"Everything's fine," he said. He could tell she wasn't convinced.

"Nothing strange is bothering you?" she asked. "Nothing," he said, shifting uncomfortably in his chair.

What if she didn't believe him because she knew something about the monsters? Did she know if the monsters were real? Had she called on them somehow? What if she was some kind of witch, capable of conjuring demons?

He looked into her eyes, but he couldn't detect any answers there. He was probably being silly and too suspicious. She was just a concerned teacher.

"If there is anything bothering you, and you want to talk about it," she said, "I want you to know you can come to me, Derek. Okay?"

"Sure."

"Okay, get out of here. It's summer."

"Right."

He slid out of the chair and almost stumbled on his way to the door. He fought an inclination to run as he stepped through her doorway, walking calmly from the building. They were going to have to check her out. They were going to have to check a lot of things out.

He was finding it harder and harder to remain convinced there weren't any monsters in Pembrook.

The game started slowly that afternoon. The players were almost reluctant to get going, and so the action moved slowly for the first few rounds.

"Will you guys get with it?" Geoff asked impatiently. "The game is harmless."

"It just seems eerie," Paige said. "I can't quit thinking it's my fault."

"It's not your fault," Geoff said. "You didn't do anything but play a game. You didn't go push her down or anything." His face reddened slightly.

She nodded. "I guess you're right." She picked up a game tile and marked a position on the board. "Okay, Vapor is on the move."

Derek listened to her moves, and then his turn came. The eerie feeling returned as he described Ogre's movements. It was almost as if he was looking at Ogre again, watching him move. He could see the fierce glow in his eyes, and the sensation of malevolence was almost overwhelming.

As he moved the tile he had chosen to represent his creature, he couldn't help feeling Ogre was really out there somewhere. Why did he feel that? It couldn't be real.

The death was an accident, the dog was killed by some wild animal. That was all. Monsters couldn't be real.

The decision to wrap up didn't come too soon for him, but at least he made it through without going into some blind panic. He had to get under control. He couldn't let himself slip over the edge into some fantasy world.

After the game, he and Paige went bike riding, and he told her about his discussion with Ms. Stone. "What do you think?" he asked.

"Maybe she's just interested."

"But she's strange. What if she knows something? What if she's behind something with our game?"

"You mean getting into our thoughts, conjuring the monsters?"

She'd almost read his mind. "Yeah. I mean, she knew about the game. Could she be doing something psychic or whatever?"

"I don't know," she said.

"What do we do about them?" he asked. "If they are real?"

"We've got to figure out where they're coming from," Paige said. "That's the first step toward an answer."

Later that afternoon, Derek sat watching the clock, waiting for his mother to show up as the minutes ticked past five. She didn't make it home until almost six, so he'd had time to think everything over. Some new questions had arisen in his mind. He wanted to know more about Neil.

After all, he'd just sort of turned up in their lives a short time ago. They had no idea where he'd come from.

Neil had probably sensed from the beginning Derek wasn't comfortable around him. That could explain him trying to be so friendly, because he knew if he was to make time with Derek's mother he'd have to get along with Derek.

Derek wondered how far he was willing to go to get what he wanted, however. He hadn't seen Neil with spellbooks under his arms, but that didn't mean the man didn't have secrets.

Maybe the fear of Neil was irrational, even subconscious. Maybe he hadn't trusted anyone his mom had ever dated because he felt protective of her since he'd been the man of the family for so long, but that didn't change the fact that he knew nothing of Neil's background. Why was he so old and not married? Why was he so willing to take on a woman who had an almost-grown son?

There might be plenty of answers, but he needed to know what they were.

He waited until his mother had come in and changed into some jeans and a comfortable tee shirt before he tried striking up a conversation.

"How was your day?" she asked after he'd made it apparent he was willing to talk.

"It was okay. I went to the workshop, then rode bikes with Paige."

"You like her?"

"Yeah. She's great."

"Don't let her break your heart," Mrs. Cliver warned. "You're both young."

"I know. I know," Derek said. "It's just fun stuff, for the summer. Hey, you have to be careful, too."

"I'm a little older than you are."

"Yeah, but how much do you know about Neil?"

"Neil's a great guy. You really need to give him a chance, Derek. I know it's difficult for you, but every guy I date isn't going to turn into Jack the Ripper."

"You've had some real losers."

"I've made some bad choices. I admit that, but it's hard to find nice men these days. And you have to remember, Neil wants to be your friend. He's not trying to take your dad's place in your heart. Deep down, I think that's part of what bothers you."

"It's not just that, Mom."

How did he tell her he'd been analyzing some things? How did he explain there might be monsters about and that he needed to check Neil out because Neil had seemed too interested in the game. That didn't make him guilty, but that certainly made him an eligible suspect.

Maybe Neil's curiosity had just been good-natured, but things hadn't started getting strange until after he knew about the game. Maybe things would have turned weird regardless, but Derek couldn't help but find that coincidence suspicious.

There were so many questions. How did Derek ask his mom?

There was no way. If he asked her too many questions, she'd only decide he was jealous of Neil. She wouldn't take him seriously.

Not unless he could somehow prove the monsters weren't make-believe.

Chapter Thirteen

The Vacant Lot

Joseph Stanley cruised his father's Jaguar off the roadway, easing the car carefully between the trees on the vacant lot until it was slightly obscured by low-hanging branches and shadows. No one driving by would notice.

He killed the engine and listened to the sigh of the cooling sounds, then turned to Suzi in the passenger seat. "This quiet enough for you?" he asked.

"Better than the Study Hall."

They had been at the teen club, which had been named with tongue firmly in cheek, but Suzi had not liked the band playing that evening, and she was depressed about Denise as well.

To console her, Joseph had suggested a drive. He'd borrowed his old man's car after the experience on the street. He didn't want a repeat of that. He'd been looking over his shoulder ever since, and frequently he felt the short hairs on the back of his neck stand up, as if something were behind him … watching.

He looked cautiously over the seat now, just to make sure all was well.

Suzi hadn't argued about the drive. She wanted something to take her mind off everything, and now she leaned over to rest her head on his shoulder, closing her eyes.

"You want to hear the radio?" he asked.

"Won't that run the battery down?"

"Not if we just play it a few minutes."

He turned it on and dialed to KWYN. They were playing songs she liked better than those at the club.

"Not bad," she said, edging even closer to Joseph. He put an arm around her and then bent forward, pressing his lips to hers. She tilted her head back, sighing slightly as she slid her arms around him.

A second later she jerked back, as if his lips had suddenly become hot. He thought he had done something and looked at her with a wrinkle in his dark eyebrows. As he studied her expression, he realized it wasn't him.

Her eyes were filled with fear. "Did you hear something?" she asked.

"Yeah, the radio."

"Turn it down," she said.

"What?"

"Turn it down."

He obeyed, twisting the knob to the left to shut out the music. The night seemed to be silent, but his heart pounded. Had the thing from the other day returned?

"It's probably just the engine," he said, trying to convince himself. He didn't want her to think he was a wimp. "It is getting kind of hot in here. You want me to roll down a window?"

"No!"

Actually he was glad at her response.

She turned in her seat so that she could look out the rear window. "I think someone is out there."

"Maybe somebody looking for a cheap thrill," he said. "Maybe one of geeks has a crush on you or something."

"I don't know," Suzi whispered. "It sounded like a cough. Or a growl."

Somewhere outside a twig snapped.

Suzi twisted in her seat to look out the side window, and a scream issued from her lips. Joseph jerked around, ready to face whatever she saw. He almost fainted with relief when he realized nothing was there.

"You're just nervous," he said as the fear slowly diminished. For a second he'd expected something to attack. "Relax. Nobody will catch us here," he said.

He put his arm around her again, and reaching forward with his free hand, he tilted her chin up slightly so that he could kiss her again.

She didn't pull away this time, and the kiss lasted for several seconds.

It ended only when the fur-covered arm shot through the glass on the passenger-side, shattering the window. Suzi screamed again, louder and louder this time.

The claw was reaching for Joseph's throat.

Chapter Fourteen

Seeing Red

Paige called about mid-evening to report to Derek what she'd heard in a television news bulletin. "They're speculating that it was a bear."

Derek held the telephone handset tightly to keep from dropping it. "Both of them?"

"Joseph and Suzi. Mauled, they said."

"Unbelievable."

"Do you think it was a bear? They were parked on the vacant lot, the same place we found the dog."

"I don't know. Maybe it was a bear that got the dog, but that's such a populated area. How would a bear get there? And why would it attack people?"

"Doesn't make sense. But the alternative's pretty strange, too."

"The alternative. You mean that it sounds like the work of ..."

"Ogre," she whispered, completing his thought for him.

"We're going to have to find a way to prove there are monsters," he whispered into the phone. "That's the only way people will believe us."

"Have you got any ideas?"

"We've got to find them somehow."

"I have a camera. I haven't used it in ages, but if we could get a snapshot, that would help. My parents are never going to let me out of the house at night, though. They heard the broadcast."

"My mom wouldn't be too keen on the idea, either. But I can get out of here once she dozes off. If we take the bikes we can move quietly."

"I guess I can sneak out, too," Paige said after thinking it over a minute. "I may have to bribe my brother, Robby, or maybe he'll be cool if I explain I'm coming to meet you."

"What time?" Derek asked.

"Midnight or so?"

"I guess that's best."

"Uh, Derek."

"Yeah."

"Will we be able to get away from them if they spot us?"

"Let's hope we won't need to."

He thought about rounding up Alex and Geoff as well, but he decided against that. Having a crowd wandering around on monster patrol might only complicate things.

When midnight struck, he checked his mom and found she was sound asleep, her book resting across her stomach. She wouldn't be moving for a while.

Wearing baggy black jeans and a black tee shirt he hoped would let him blend in with the night, he slipped out the back door, walked around the house for his bike for a silent escape, and headed for Paige's.

He was glad to find her waiting for him at the end of her driveway. She too had dressed in dark clothes, and her hair was pulled into a ponytail. She had her camera on a strap around her neck. She'd also managed to scrounge up a flashlight, which would probably come in handy.

"Where do we go?" she asked.

"To the woods, I guess. I mean they wouldn't linger on the lot, would they? They'd go back to their lair."

"I don't know. Is this a suicide mission?"

"I hope not."

"Is this a stupid mission?"

"Let's hope so," Derek said. "It's only stupid if there are no monsters. Or maybe it's stupid because there are monsters."

Climbing back onto their bikes, they rode side by side through the residential streets. Everything was quiet in Pembrook at this hour until the loud roaring sound came from behind them.

Derek looked back over his shoulder to see two white-hot orbs bearing down on them.

Headlights, he realized with relief as an old Chevy Nova with a group of loud guys in their late teens sped by.

By the time they reached the wood, they were practically trembling.

"It sounded like a better idea than it feels," Paige observed, edging her bike's kickstand down with her toe.

"You've got a point," Derek agreed.

She handed him the flashlight. "You handle this, I'll handle the camera," she suggested.

Accepting the light, he turned it on and looked at the bulb. It was dimmer than he expected.

"It's all we had," Paige said.

"It'll have to do."

Leaving the shoulder of the road, they moved cautiously toward the woods, holding hands to comfort each other. Somehow it seemed safer to be holding on to someone.

A gun would have felt even more comfortable, Derek speculated, but he didn't know anyone who owned one.

Moonlight offered illumination as they neared the trees. That proved fortunate. The flash-light beam stretched only a short distance into the darkness. The combination of the two at least allowed some visibility.

"It looks a lot spookier at night than it did in the daytime," Paige said. "And that's saying something. In daylight it reminded me of a Clive Barker movie."

"It'll be okay," Derek said. "Just be ready to run."

"I'm sure I'll move pretty fast with a monster after me, but if they're anything like our characters they're superhuman."

"I never said this wasn't dangerous," Derek said. "If you had, I would've argued."

At the edge of the wood, they paused, steeling themselves. Wandering through a forest in the dark would've been a foolhardy endeavor on any occasion. Entering a stretch of wood where there might be monsters was lunacy.

"We're stupid for doing this," Derek said. "What if our imaginations are just working in overdrive? What if the monsters aren't responsible?"

Paige squeezed his hand tightly. "What if it's not our imagination, and what if they get more kids? This is the best way we can find to start getting to the bottom of things."

"You're right," Derek said. "Keep prodding me so I don't turn back."

Still clasping hands, they moved onward, retracing the same path they had followed on the scouting expedition. Having worked with the maps of the area daily since that excursion, they were more familiar with the area than they might have been. That made it slightly easier to weave through the trees.

Derek aimed the flashlight into corners and along branches, searching for some hint of movement or some gleam of eyes that might indicate one of the monsters.

"We're going to have to find Ogre or the Feline, or whatever," Paige said. "A picture of Vapor won't convince anybody."

"You've got a good point," Derek said. "It does occur to me if any of the monsters get to us out here, people will be convinced there's a problem of some kind, picture or not. They may still think it's a bear, but at least they'd take action."

"I'm not really thrilled with the idea of dying for a noble cause," Paige said.

"Me either. I was just trying to look at the bright side."

"The bright side is that we didn't have more people in our club," she said. "Then the whole county would be in trouble."

Derek, enjoying the challenge of matching her retorts, was about to respond when the flashlight beam swept across a cluster of bushes up ahead.

The light reflected off two green orbs—eyes this time!

Derek realized the eyes of a cat, dog, or raccoon would have been smaller than the twin circles ahead of them. He wanted to forget about pictures and convincing people and everything else. Safety seemed the main concern for the moment.

Only the grip of Paige's hand kept him from bolting, and he could tell the same was true for her. At least they were helping each other. Maybe they could get the job done.

Snapping off the light, he pushed Paige off the trail. They ducked behind a tree and crouched, waiting for the owner of the eyes to make some movement.

It came in a few seconds. Leaves rustled, and then there were footfalls.

The steps were quick and deliberate, and as their eyes slowly adjusted to the darkness, Derek and Paige began to make out the outline of something in the shadows.

Derek had never quite understood what people meant by feeling their hearts stop, but suddenly it became clear. His heart seemed about to freeze as he watched the catlike creature burst through the tall grass, its head darting from side to side.

It was everything they had imagined the Feline to be as they had played, and Derek was surprised just how terrifying it could be to lay eyes on something that should not exist.

That violation of reality seemed almost as frightening as his imaginings of what the monster might do to him.

Carefully, Paige readied her camera, and, keeping low, they moved slowly through the brush, trailing the creature, waiting for an opportunity to get a focus on him.

The size of the monster was startling. It was practically as tall as a man, its legs long and powerful, allowing it to walk partially upright. The head was broad and heavy looking. The teeth would be even worse than Derek had imagined, long and sharp, curved daggers.

"He's going to smell us if the breeze changes," Paige whispered.

"I know," Derek said. "Let's just be as careful as we can."

They scrambled onward, keeping as quiet as they could as the Feline continued its hunt. It was either looking for food or searching for the other monsters, a frightening proposition.

Derek kept watching for signs of mist, and any disturbance made him consider the possibility that Ogre was bearing down on them. If the Feline was real, those others had to be out here as well, and Tyger, too.

He half wished one of them would appear. Then they could flash the snapshot and get on with the business of running for their lives.

Taking a picture was certainly going to alert the creatures of their whereabouts. Then they would be left to try and escape. He wished they'd taken more time for planning, but hopefully their knowledge of the wood would help them escape.

"He's slowing down some," Paige whispered.

Ahead of them, the cat creature was pausing near a tree, its bushy tail swaying back and forth. Derek half thought he was dreaming or at least looking at some mechanical monster from a movie. It didn't look just like a big cat. It was lean and swift in its movements, quicker than a cat.

When it wheeled around with a screech-like cry, he was convinced it wasn't an illusion. Its eyes blazed wide in the flashlight beam, and the mouth opened, revealing the horrible fangs.

The creature's front paws raised quickly, the claws extending like rows of knives.

Paige snapped a quick picture, and the suddenness of the flash caused the Feline to turn, its eyes seared by the bulb.

When it did, he grabbed Paige's hand, and they charged, scurrying as fast as they could in the underbrush. To confuse the cat, they plunged deeper into the forest, then curved behind trees and began to work their way back toward the roadway.

They avoided the trail, which would be too obvious a route, and half-running, half-leaping, made their way over as much of the debris and tangles as they could.

With the sound of their own breathing and the rustle and crash around them, they quickly lost track of the Feline's position.

"He could be anywhere," Paige said when they paused, crouching beside an oak tree.

Derek looked up into the branches above them and was glad to see they were empty.

He almost found it impossible to believe they were hiding in the dark, trying to avoid being ripped to shreds by an oversized housecat.

"It's like being trapped in a cartoon," he said.

"Yeah, and we're the mice. Are you sure we're headed back toward the road?"

"It's a little easier when you're looking at a map in the living room. All these trees look alike, but I think we're heading right."

They edged from beneath the tree and gazed skyward, trying to view enough of the sky to get bearings from the stars. Neither of them could remember which way the Big Dipper pointed, however.

They had to rely on instinct, and after a couple more seconds of gasping air, they started off again, running and jumping with all they could muster.

The sound behind them became audible in a few seconds. Something was pursuing, thrashing through the brush at a high rate of speed.

"It's coming," Paige said between breaths.

"Let's keep going. If he gets close we'll split and confuse him."

"If he eats me, will you remember me?"

"Sure."

Branches and bushes tore at them, and Derek felt a thorn of some kind pierce his shirt. For a second, he thought it was a cat claw, and panic had almost overtaken him before his brain registered reality.

The Feline was still a few yards behind them but closing. It was geared better for travel through the forest. It was a monster.

"Spilt," Derek decided, and they parted, putting distance between them while still moving in the same direction they'd been headed. If they could get to the roadway and the bikes, they had a chance.

Derek hadn't run so hard since P.E., and he discovered he couldn't maintain the pace he had originally set. He wondered how Paige was doing. He'd heard girls actually ran faster than boys. For her sake he prayed that was true.

The Feline was as fast as a gazelle. Ahead of him, he began to see signs of light. Maybe he was going to make it.

He ducked his head and ran harder, faster, driving himself forward, willing his legs to propel him even though the muscles ached.

Finally, he pushed through a cluster of brush and burst from the trees, the movement suddenly easier without obstacles. He raised his head to look for his bicycle, and his vision was blurred, filled with a color—red.

Bright red.

Chapter Fifteen

Scare

The lights from the state police cruiser were as bright as spotlights, or at least they seemed to be. Derek raised his forearm in front of his face to shield his eyes as the red waves glared through the bubbles atop the car.

Paige stood near the passenger door, hysterically trying to explain to the cop what had happened. The young blond officer had a face made of stone. He showed no expression, but as Derek rushed up, he turned and looked at him with a hard stare.

"This boy bother you?" the cop asked.

"No. He was with me. I'm telling you, there was this animal, a monster," Paige blurted out.

She'd snatched the photograph from the camera, and she presented it to him now.

"This is just a blur, ma'am," the cop said, handing it back to her. "We did have some kids killed earlier this evening, but that was a good distance away. You don't need to be out wandering around."

She looked at Derek, and they both turned to glance nervously through the trees. The lights seemed to have driven the creature away, or at least it didn't want to come out of the wood and be spotted.

"It was there," Derek said.

"I don't have time for Stephen King stories, son," the cop said. "The young lady's parents were worried about her. Two other kids are dead. You two don't need to be out here."

"My parents called you?"

"They called the Pembrook police, actually. I just happened to be cruising when I heard the radio broadcast and spotted your bikes. I need to take you two home. It's really late and we don't know what got those other kids."

"Maybe we should go back and take our chances with that thing," Paige whispered to Derek as the bikes were loaded into the police car trunk. "My folks are going to make the Feline look like Pee Wee Herman. They think I'm still a child, obviously."

Paige's expression hadn't improved much by workshop time the next morning. She stood at one end of the gym with her arms folded, and the way the muscle in her jaw rippled Derek worried she was going to crush her teeth.

"Your parents didn't take it too well?" he asked.

"Not very," she said. "I'm lucky they didn't behead me."

"My mom told me she didn't want a police cruiser bringing me home again," Derek said, and smiled. "At least we survived, even if we didn't come back with something other people could believe."

"Yeah, but now I'm practically grounded, and my folks want me to cut back on playing the game."

"That's going to make it hard to try and figure out what's going on," Derek said.

"I know. We saw a real monster of some kind and they're worried about ... arrrhhh. I could spit nails."

They were still discussing a strategy a few minutes later when Alex and Geoff came walking across the gym.

"You guys heard what happened?" Alex asked. He sounded worried.

"Yeah, and we had some problems of our own last night," Derek said.

"Did you see the monsters?" Geoff asked, his tone suggesting he was half joking.

"Actually we did," Derek said. He turned to Paige. "Did you bring the picture?"

She pulled it from the pocket of her shorts and passed it over to Alex. Geoff craned his neck to get a look at the frame as well. His nose wrinkled.

"It's blurry," he said, sinking his hands into the pockets of his baggy jeans. "It's as bad as that film footage of Bigfoot or the pictures of Nessy."

"Who?" Derek asked. -

"That's what they call the Loch Ness monsters," Alex said. "I have to agree this is pretty blurry. It kind of looks like the Feline, but you could've done this by getting up real close to a housecat."

"We didn't have a lot of time to check the lighting and shutter speed," Paige said. "Besides, it's an automatic camera."

Alex shrugged and handed it back to her. "Didn't convince your parents?"

"We didn't bother," she said. Briefly they explained what had happened.

"Now I guess you guys don't believe us either," she said.

"Hey, don't get mad at me," Alex protested. "I'm hearing you out. I just don't know if our monsters are to blame."

"Joseph and Suzi were torn up by something," Derek said.

"Maybe it was just a wild animal," Geoff said. "I just don't know what to make of it. I mean, how would our game come to life?"

Paige pointed at him. "What if the game materials had something to do with it?"

"This started happening after they showed up," Derek said. "I can remember how I started feeling weird after that."

"They're just pieces of paper," Alex said.

"But remember how they glowed?" Derek said. "I never really saw that," Alex said.

"It was a trick of the light," Geoff interjected.

"They glowed," Paige said. "A trick of the light wouldn't be Day-Glo green. What if they didn't come from the magazine? And think about it. We've had them with us in our game packets every time we've played."

"It's enough to seem weird," Derek said.

"Where would they have come from? They looked official," Alex said.

"Different people have seen us with the game," Derek recalled. "We've had the materials out at school and different places, and we've talked about it a lot, even in public places. Somebody who understands sorcery could've figured out how to sabotage our game."

"Sabotage our game with sorcery?" Alex asked with a shake of his head. "Listen to yourself."

"Anything could be possible here," Derek said. "Who knows who could be behind it? We've got to figure out what's going on, whether the answer seems rational or not. More people could die."

"Well, since we're scared to play the game, we can play detective," Alex said. "Not!"

"What if things get worse," Derek said. "What if somebody else gets hurt, and it's because of our game. Then we're responsible. I don't like the snobs, but I don't want something I came up with destroying them."

Alex remained skeptical. "What have we got? A blurred picture, visions you guys had which could be active imaginations at work, and some freak accidents. That's not a lot of evidence."

"But we saw the thing last night," Paige said. "It wasn't active imagination. We had to run for our lives. Look, maybe if I'd really believed it was real I wouldn't have gone out there last night, even knowing about Joseph and Suzi. But whatever doubts I had got canceled."

Before conversation could continue, Ms. Stone walked to center stage and shouted across the gym, calling for the kids to gather for the day's activities. She gave a brief lecture on the deaths and explained that the workshop would continue, though she could understand if anyone wanted to drop out.

Derek looked at the snobs' table. Craig was the only one who'd made it. Amber was probably too upset to attend today.

Derek was still trying to come up with answers for himself when he was called on midway through the period, and even though he had not really prepared his work, he managed to do an impressive job with the piece he'd been assigned. He poured emotion into it, and the class applauded when he was finished.

For a few seconds, as he took a bow, he forgot about his problems, but only for a few seconds. Thoughts of the monsters returned as he walked between the rows of tables back toward his seat.

When class finally ended, he was almost shuddering as he contemplated Pembrook overrun by monsters. Could it happen? He and Paige waved good-bye to their friends and watched the other kids depart.

"I think our first step is to figure out if those runes are real," Derek said as he and Paige walked toward his car.

"How do we do that?"

"Let's call *Scare* and find out if we're really winners."

He drove them back to his house, and after he'd fixed a couple of peanut butter and jelly sandwiches, he dialed information.

After the phone had rung a couple of times, he got a switchboard operator and asked to speak to someone about the Terror Club. He was put on hold.

"What did they say?" Paige asked.

"That I had to wait."

A few moments later, a click sounded over the line, and then he heard someone pick up.

"Contest director," a man's voice said.

Derek motioned Paige over so that they could share the earpiece.

"I was trying to get some information on your Terror Club game," Derek said.

"Look, winners will be announced as soon as…"

"You haven't sent out the contest winners yet?"

"Not yet. We're swamped. I've got an office piled high with entries, and I'm trying to sift through them now."

"Would someone who entered a monster have received a packet with some game materials?" Derek asked.

"Not from us. We haven't even finished preparing our response to entrants. I'm sorry, but it's a little early. More people entered than we anticipated. Just keep watching. You should hear something from us soon."

"Okay, thanks."

Derek put the phone down softly.

"Now we know," he said. "It wasn't *Scare* that responded."

"Then who did those things come from?" Paige asked.

"If we could figure that out, I guess we'd know where the monsters were coming from," Derek said. "So we have to find out who sent us the packets."

"Yeah, but that won't be easy."

"Let's just keep calm," Paige said. "We have to be careful."

"We're talking about monsters maybe attacking the whole town. If things follow through, if they keep attacking people we've been mad at, they'll probably go after Amber and Craig next. Who knows where they'll go after that? Anybody that makes us angry could be in danger."

Paige's eyes revealed her fear. "Let's get together with Alex and Geoff and see what they think," she said.

"Aren't you grounded?"

"This is a little more important than that."

When they arrived at Alex's, they found Geoff was already there. They were in the back room looking over some of Alex's old comic books.

Quickly Derek explained the results of the call to *Scare*.

"Okay, so we got phony packages in the mail," Alex said. "What does that mean?"

"That somebody wanted to manipulate our game."

"But who?"

"That's what we've got to figure out," Derek said. "But we also have to figure out a way to stop the monsters from doing it again."

Opening his game folder, Derek unfolded his rune and looked it over top to bottom for some sign of a printer's mark or copyright notice. He didn't find any indication of where the materials might have come from. The tiles also offered no answers.

"Looks like we're stuck," Alex said. "And there are monsters in the woods."

Derek looked again at his rune and almost jumped out of his chair. It was glowing again, this time bright green.

Chapter Sixteen

Where's Alex?

After discussion, they decided coming up with answers would take teamwork. Alex and Geoff agreed to check at the library to see if they could find information on the occult, while Paige and Derek decided to go to the local print shops to determine if the runes had been printed there.

The first stop was downtown at the Ink Blot. Derek drove, observing speed limits even though he wanted to put the pedal down.

The Ink Blot was one of two shops in Pembrook, a small operation run by a woman named Tori Winters. She was about thirty-five with dark hair, and she handled her business with only a couple of assistants.

"What can I do for you?" she asked when they entered the front door.

Derek showed her his game packet, which he had retrieved from his house. "Could you do something like this?" he asked.

He and Paige had agreed that if they just walked in and asked if the materials had been printed at her shop, she might be reluctant to talk. Some of the acting skills they'd developed in Ms. Stone's class were going to be useful.

"It would be tough, and expensive," she said. "That's an odd color of ink. I don't know if I could match it. The paper would be hard to come by. I'm not sure what bond it is, and those markings are not traditional fonts. It would be a very tough job."

Derek nodded. That didn't rule out anything. Neil had a good job and could afford high print costs. That wouldn't get Neil convicted in court, but he kept remembering that things had been normal until Neil had talked to him about the game.

100

His life had been normal until Neil had shown up. Maybe he just suspected Neil because he didn't like him, but maybe he didn't like Neil because deep down the guy had something to hide. He was worth checking out.

He held up the paper. "Have you ever done anything like this?" he asked.

Miss Winters shook her head. "Afraid not. What is it for? Some kind of game?"

"A role-playing game," Paige said. "These are really set decorations. We made one up ourselves, more or less, so we need something like this for all the players."

The woman shook her head. "I don't think I could do it without charging you pretty high. I'm sorry," she said.

"Well, we were just checking," Derek said, folding the papers back together and stuffing them in his envelope.

Before they made it to the door, Miss Winters called out, "I could try calling Type World for you."

Derek and Paige looked at each other and nodded. Type World was in a shopping center on the far side of town. This would save a long drive.

With a smile, Miss Winters picked up the phone and dialed. "Jill, this is Nelda Winters. How are you?"

A few moments of polite conversation passed before she asked about the printing job. She nodded as she continued to talk. Derek and Paige strained to hear the voice on the other end, but they couldn't. They had to wait agonizing minutes for Miss Winters to hang up.

"She did something that sounds like what you've got there," Miss Winters said. "A man called her about the job. She said it was a little weird. He sent his samples in by courier and then had the materials delivered to a post office box. He paid in cash. She says she can do the job, though. These must be like the ones she printed."

"Thanks a lot," Derek said. "You've really helped us out."

They kept smiling as they headed for the door, but the grins faded once they were outside.

"I hated doing things that way," Paige said.

"It was the only way," Derek said. "We had to find out."

"Yeah, at least we got information. What do you think?"

"A man called. That could have been Neil."

"It could have been any man."

"Maybe, but you know I don't trust Neil."

"You're not exactly an objective observer," Paige pointed out.

"Maybe not, but he makes a good suspect."

"Why? Because you don't like the idea of his dating your mom? I'm not trying to argue. I'm just trying to be realistic."

"I am being realistic. Neil likes my mom. He knows I don't like him. What if he wants to get me out of the way?"

"He's making a big effort."

"Think about it. A man ordered the printing. It would be easy for him to send someone from his office with the materials he wanted, and he could've set up a post office box under a fake name to get the material."

"Should we go talk to him?" Paige said. "Confront him?"

"Maybe he'd be less likely to do something to us if we're at his office," Derek agreed.

Fortunately, Neil's office wasn't as far away as Type World. It was only a few blocks from the Ink Blot, in fact, and they made the trip quickly.

The building was new with ornate wrought-iron decorating the red brick. A couple of offices occupied the space. Neil's was through a white door just off the entryway. Derek and Paige again put on their smiles and walked in.

A secretary sat behind a counter that looked like a roadblock, but she agreed to call back and tell Neil it was Derek.

As Derek expected, Neil agreed to see them. He wanted to appear to be Derek's buddy, after all. He wouldn't turn down an opportunity to be courteous. They were shown back to his large, paneled office. He was at his desk, leaning over some paperwork, when they stepped through his door.

He looked up with a smile. "Hi, folks. What brings you along?"

"We were in the neighborhood."

"Not much in this neighborhood but offices," Neil said.

"We were sightseeing," Derek answered. Then he pulled out the folded set of runes and placed them on the desk.

"Do these look familiar?"

"No. Wait a minute, aren't they from your game?"

"You're sure you don't recognize them?" Derek asked. "They were printed locally. A courier dropped them over at Type World. They were mailed to a post office box."

Neil smiled. "I really don't know what you're talking about," he said.

Derek looked across the desk at him, watching his eyes, studying his expression. He seemed genuinely perplexed. Sure he'd be set to deny any involvement, but he didn't seem to be lying.

He seemed amused more than anything, as if he thought Derek was playing some kind of joke.

"You don't know anything about runes?" Derek asked.

"Not any more than you've told me. Did your mom put you up to this?"

"No." Derek bowed his head. "We thought you might be playing a joke on us."

"With these?"

"Yes. They didn't come from the game company."

"Derek, you're not still chasing monsters, are you? Your mom mentioned your escapade."

"We're trying to find answers," Derek protested.

"Is it me? Are you trying to get rid of me, Derek? I don't mean you any harm. I'm still hoping you and I can be friends."

Paige reached over and took Derek's hand, squeezing for support.

"How do I know you're not after something else?"

"Derek, I'm not involved with runes or monster games. Believe me. Dealing with my clients is enough of a nightmare."

Slowly Derek nodded. "I guess we made a mistake. I'm sorry we didn't trust you."

Still holding Paige's hand, he walked with her toward the door. They paused before making an exit. "Don't mention this to Mom," he said.

"I won't, but you need to talk to her, Derek."

"I guess I do."

He bowed his head again and heaved a heavy sigh as they stepped into the hallway.

"He thinks I'm deranged," Derek said.

"Is he telling the truth?"

"He seems to be, but if he's not behind all this, who is?"

"Ms. Stone? She could've had the printing done just as easily as Neil."

Derek felt his thoughts swirling, as if they were spinning and jamming against each other. "I don't know who to believe anymore," he said.

"Calm down," Paige said softly. "We'll just keep working."

"There are monsters out there," Derek protested. "How much time do you think we have?"

Gently she took his hand. "Panicking isn't going to do any good. Let's go back to your house and figure out our next move. I still have a while before I need to go home. We ought to be able to figure something out."

Her words helped him get control of the tension that was trying to claim him. Somehow she made it sound possible. He couldn't imagine how they were going to solve this mystery, but he was glad to have Paige's comfort along the way.

When they made it back to his house, they began going over the game materials again, looking for some other kind of clue.

"There's nothing here," Derek decided after they had examined each piece of paper twice.

'We could go and talk to the people at the other typesetter, find out what the courier looked like," Paige suggested.

"We're going to have to do that."

Further words were cut off by the ringing of the telephone.

It rang a second time before they recovered from the shock of the sudden sound. Derek scrambled for the handset before the caller could hang up. It might be his mom with dinner suggestions or a complaint about his bothering Neil if she'd heard about the visit. That didn't matter. It might also be Alex with some news or …

It was Mrs. Jackson, and she sounded worried. "What's wrong?" he asked.

"Have you heard from Alex lately?"

"Not since early afternoon," Derek said.

"I expected him back by now."

"I guess he should have been home by now He was going to the library," Derek said. "He and Geoff were going to do some research."

"So Geoff could be missing, too?"

"If they're not at the library. Did you try to call Geoff's house?"

"I tried Paige's. I couldn't find a listing for Geoff's family."

Derek's eyes widened, and he looked at Paige who looked back expectantly.

"No number or address?"

"You don't know where he lives?"

"We've never been there. I guess I never thought about it really."

"What's going on?" Paige asked.

"Something weird," he said. "We'll go check the library and see if they're there."

"Let me know if you find them. I'm sure everything is fine, but I'm just a little worried."

Paige was talking before he could put down the phone. "We've never thought about Geoff, but we don't know anything about him."

"That's true. He seems harmless, but he is kind of weird."

"Could Geoff be evil? We really don't know where he lives. Maybe he's had some reason to always make an excuse to keep from using his house or going to his house."

"Alex hasn't come home yet. His mom got worried ..."

"I picked up on that. What about Geoff? Think."

"This all started around the time Geoff showed up, and he was the one who was so anxious to get us all involved in the game."

"He did kind of spearhead things," Paige agreed.

"He was the one who wanted to explore the woods, too, and he was the one who kept everything rolling," Derek said.

Paige's eyes almost popped from the sockets. "Re-member how the birds attacked him out there. Not us, just him."

"Maybe the birds knew something," Derek said. "We've got to find out," Paige urged. "Before he hurts Alex."

"If he hasn't already," Derek said.

Together they rushed for the door.

Chapter Seventeen

Headstones

Derek did speed this time, pressing the gas pedal hard as the car screeched over to the library. The parking lot was full, so he slid the Mustang into a No Parking zone, and they headed inside.

The reading room was filled with people who sat at various tables or sat on a couple of sofas near the wall and perused newspapers and magazines. Alex and Derek weren't in sight.

Quickly Paige and Derek rushed back to the stacks, moving in and out of the rows of shelves until they'd searched all of them. Alex and Geoff were nowhere in the building.

"Why didn't we think about Geoff?" Paige asked. "We should have been suspicious. He never talked about parents or anything."

"He seems so harmless," Derek said. "Just a little guy who wasn't too mature yet."

"But a guy clever enough to call a print firm and disguise his voice, then go by himself claiming to be a courier."

"That has to be how he did that," Derek agreed. "But it still doesn't make sense. Why? What's he up to?"

"Maybe it was just for the excitement, or the power. Maybe he hated the snobs worse than we did."

"This is getting weirder and weirder," Derek said. "I guess our next stop is the Nightmare Wood."

"That's got to be where he went," Paige said. "That's where he wanted us to play our game."

They climbed into Derek's car again and made the trip over to the woods. It wasn't that far away, but afternoon was dragging down when they arrived.

Standing side by side, they looked through the trees, searching for signs of life in the shadows of the oaks and pines. Only leaves and needles touched by the afternoon breeze seemed to be moving.

"If they're in there, they've moved toward the back," Derek said.

"To the cemetery?"

"Probably. Maybe that's the reason he chose the wood," Derek speculated.

"Maybe."

"What if the monsters are still there, too?"

"Maybe they're dormant until nightfall," Derek said. "Let's hope so."

As they had before, they stepped from the roadside and began the trek through the forest, this time using a map from one of the gaming packets. Enough sunlight still filtered down through the trees to make that possible.

As they moved, Derek felt fear tightening his chest muscles. Running from the monster had been frightening, but that had all happened fast. This fear was worse because it was constant, unrelenting. They had picked the right name for their club. This was terrifying.

He reached over and took Paige's hand, both for reassurance and to comfort her. She was trembling, every bit as frightened as he was.

About ten feet into the forest, ten slow feet, they found an oak tree with deep scratches in the bark. The ridges extended from the ground about seven feet up the trunk, deep vertical slashes.

Paige swallowed as she looked at them. "A cat sharpening its claws," she said.

"What a set of claws. That's what was chasing us!" Paige placed a hand over her heart. "This is really getting scary," she said.

"If we had time, this would be pretty good proof to show the cops," Derek said. "We can't afford to take that long now Alex could be in trouble."

"They'd only say it was a bear or something. They'd dismiss it before admitting to a giant cat-thing. It was probably only put here to scare us."

"It's effective."

After looking at the scratches a few more seconds, they moved forward, ducking a few branches and working their way deeper into the wood. The map made things a little easier, allowing them to stick to the trail and avoid some thick clusters of trees and some underbrush that would've been almost impenetrable, at least for people.

"I wonder if he's going to be in the cemetery?" Derek asked.

"I was thinking about that," Paige said. "Remember that old caretaker's cottage we saw back there? He wasn't interested in exploring that when we made our expedition. He was excited about everything else, so you'd think an old house would have caught his attention, too."

"Except he didn't want us going in there."

"Because that's where he's set up residence, I'll bet," Paige said.

"We'll have to check it out," Derek decided, adding, "Carefully."

As they moved forward, the forest seemed thicker than it had before, as if more vines and brambles had woven together to make travel more difficult. Finally they had to give up on walking upright and crouch almost to the ground to progress.

That led to the discovery of the track. Paige was inching along when she happened to notice the uncovered patch of ground. The footprint was slightly more than an inch deep and did not resemble the footprint of a human.

"It's got to be Ogre's mark," Derek said.

"Another sign to scare us."

"Or anybody else," Derek speculated. "He didn't want anybody coming back here."

"Not unannounced."

They were bathed in sweat by the time they finally emerged from the tangles and crouched in the high grass at the edge of the cemetery. Keeping as low as possible, they peered at the rows of headstones, trying to get a look back at the cabin. That proved impossible from their vantage.

"We can keep behind the headstones," Paige suggested. "That'll give us some cover."

"You're right. We need to hurry. Alex would probably hate getting eaten."

On hands and knees, they crawled from the edge of the grass and rushed toward the headstones. Ducking as they reached the first tall monument, they leaned back against it. They were breathing heavily, and the cool surface of the stone offered a soothing touch.

"Can we see the shack from here?" Derek asked.

Paige was busy pulling her hair back. It had picked up fragments of leaves and thorns, and she had no hope of clearing them out. Quickly, with a ponytail band from her pocket, she did manage to sweep it back away from her face and neck to help her keep cooler.

Then she turned with Derek, and they slid their fingers over the top of the stone and raised their heads a few inches.

They could see the cabin now, though they didn't have a good view. The front door was closed with no sign of movement noticeable.

"At least he hasn't seen us," Paige said as they settled into sitting positions.

"He's not showing it if he has."

"What are we going to do if we get closer?" she asked. "Should we go back and get weapons?"

"Let's hope my mom or your folks have missed us and will be looking for us by now, or that Alex's mom is tired of waiting for word," he said.

"What if they aren't?"

"We'll have to think of something."

Staying low, they moved on along the row of headstones, using each monument for cover. The house remained silent each time they checked it—no movement, no voices, no screams sounded from the interior.

"Maybe if we get a little closer," Paige suggested. "Let's go."

They rounded one row of stones and scrambled across the next, scrunching behind a shorter monument. It seemed less dingy than the others. Suddenly Paige realized why.

"Look at this," she said, tapping Derek's arm.

"What?" He was peering around the stone toward the house.

"The name."

Finally he turned to look, and he felt his breath catch in his chest as he stared at the chiseled lettering.

GEOFFREY NOVAK
1877–1893

"What do you suppose that means?" Derek asked. "Is he a ghost?"

"That would explain his attraction to the cemetery. If this is true, he died when he was sixteen. Like most of the other kids here."

"The age he appears to be now."

"That wouldn't explain the monsters or anything like that, though."

"I don't know what to make of it, then."

"It's what you might call a long story."

They jerked around from the stone to see Geoff. He wasn't the Geoff they'd become accustomed to, however.

The voice was deeper with a strange quality, and he had changed from the casual clothes he usually wore into a dark outfit and jacket. His hair was no longer styled in modern fashion either. It was brushed straight, and it was longer than it had previously appeared, the edges touching his collar. He also seemed more powerful than he had before.

Although he still could've passed for sixteen, he seemed much older. His eyes were dark and cold, and he held himself with strength and self-assurance.

"What are you doing?" Derek asked. "Where's Alex?"

"I was just about to take you to him," Geoff said. "If you'll walk toward the house."

In case they had any ideas about disagreeing, from his belt he produced a short knife with a narrow, pointed blade and a jeweled handle.

"He's no ghost," Paige said.

"Not a ghost, no," Geoff said. "I'm a sorcerer."

"You've got to be kidding," Derek said.

"Not at all. If you'll please move on into the house…"

The porch creaked as they stepped onto the planks, and the musty odor of decay seemed to fill their nostrils as they moved toward the front door.

Derek pushed it open as he approached, and as light spilled into the narrow front room, he saw Alex sitting on the floor near the wall. His hands and feet were bound, and his glasses had been knocked off. He seemed disoriented, but for a second his expression seemed hopeful. His hopes faded again when Geoff walked through the doorway.

"If you'll get comfortable next to your friend, we'll talk," Geoff said.

Obediently, Derek and Paige took seats, and Geoff produced some more ropes to tie them.

As he completed the task, Paige looked toward the dust-clouded window. The sun was continuing its slow descent behind a stand of trees. Even on long summer days, night had to come.

"Looks like we're in trouble," she whispered.

"He's crazy," Alex whispered back. "I was looking through some books on the occult, and he started demanding that we had to get out of the library"

"Were you getting close to something?" Derek asked.

"I guess I was. We started walking, and as soon as we got to a part of the street where there were no people around he jumped me. I never figured he could be so strong. The next thing I knew, I woke up here."

Paige told him about the headstone.

"Strange," Alex said. "I was reading about the interest in the occult that sprang up toward the end of the nineteenth century"

"The time he was supposed to have died."

"Maybe he didn't die at all," Derek said.

"Maybe it's time for you to stop whispering," Geoff said. "Whatever you figure out will not be enough to help you."

"What do you want from us?" Paige demanded. "We were your friends."

"Because I helped you with the game, helped you find something interesting to do to pass the summer days? What would've happened when school started? Would you have stayed my friends then? Or would you have ditched me for cooler people?"

"We would've stayed your friends," Alex said.

"Come on, Geoff. What's going on?"

"You'll find out. Just give it a little while."

He walked across the hardwood floor and sat down in the room's only chair, a decaying ladderback. A grin crossed his lips.

"You've been helping me," he said. "I needed your energy and your creativity."

"You were using us, in other words," Derek said. "I'm afraid so. I needed the Terror Club to make my monsters stronger."

He followed the statement with a laugh, a long, low laugh that made it clear he was insane. At that moment, Derek realized Geoff was capable of anything.

He tried to brace himself for whatever the night had in store. He felt certain it would make the Nightmare Wood worthy of its nickname.

Chapter Eighteen

Sorcerer's Apprentice

"What do you gain from all this?" Paige asked as Geoff paced nervously about the narrow space in front of them.

"More power than you could ever imagine," he said.

"So how did it all work? How did you take our thoughts and make them real?"

"It's ancient magic," he said. "As old as time. The runes were discovered in the lands which are now Germany, but they served only to channel the forces which are now at my command."

"When did you learn about it? It must've been a hundred years ago," Derek said.

"Based on what you saw on the headstone?"

Derek nodded.

"Indeed it was. My family was among the richest in Pembrook. It was a very small community back then. My father was in banking, and since he held the mortgage on most of the farms in this region, people hated him. I was a small boy, not terribly healthy. Much of the anger at him was vented on me. I endured it all because I didn't have much choice, but I looked for a way out, a way to overcome my tormentors."

"Evil magic became your answer," Alex concluded.

"Magic, period, became my answer. You've read too much Tolkien, Alex. It's not as cut and dried as good and evil."

"You decided you'd use it for evil, though," Paige said.

"You call it evil. Maybe it was justice. The summer of my fifteenth year, my father decided to take the family on a European vacation. I welcomed the trip because I knew it would allow me to be away from the children who teased me for a couple of months. Travel wasn't as rapid in those days."

"Europe was filled with spiritualists and magicians at that time," Alex said. "I read that Sir Arthur Conan Doyle was a mystic."

"Of sorts. There were many others, experienced men. I managed to get away from my parents one afternoon in London, and I wandered into a little shop where I met the man who would become my teacher—Jean Delancre. He was originally from France. He relocated due to some difficulties he had there.

"When I saw just a hint of what he could do, I decided to become his apprentice."

"A sorcerer's apprentice," Alex said. "How cute."

"Make jokes if you want. It was effective. My parents were terribly upset. They had thought of sending me to a boarding school, but my courses weren't what they'd anticipated. Mr. Delancre persuaded them, eventually."

"You stayed long enough to learn magic," Paige said. "Then you came back, didn't you?"

"What makes you say that?"

"So many of those headstones belong to young people who died about a hundred years ago. You came home and got revenge on the kids who picked on you."

Geoff laughed again. "The pieces are beginning to fall into place for you," he said.

"But I don't understand why your grave is out there," Derek said.

"When the children started dying, my parents realized what was going on. They didn't want their name marred by people learning their son was the cause of the deaths, so they sent me on a trip and announced that I had died abroad. They had a coffin shipped in from somewhere and buried it out there without ever opening it."

"That doesn't explain why you're back," Paige asked.

"It's the anniversary," Geoff said. "After such a long time, I decided to return to my hometown and see what new things I could accomplish.

My monsters, the ones you helped me create, will allow me to destroy Pembrook's children all over again."

"But most of the kids here now haven't done anything to you," Derek said. "They're totally innocent."

"Are they? The snobs? Have they treated me any differently?"

"We've been your friends," Paige said. "All of us."

"Because I made you want to be my friend. That's the only reason. But you've served your purpose. All of you are the descendants of those who lived then, even you, Paige. You didn't even know you had ancestors from Pembrook, did you? Your families were among the ones who survived.

"It was only fitting that you should be of help to me. The game Derek was planning when I met you proved to be useful. Through it, you've all provided the mental energy to make my monsters strong, just like I wanted. Your anger at the snobs helped channel the monsters, and when they drew blood they became even more powerful. They can function on their own now. They have become more real with each round of the game; now they can function independently. It's time they were unleashed. They can finish off Craig and Amber, and then they can overrun the town."

"You don't want to hurt so many innocent people," Alex protested.

"I want to hurt everybody," Geoff said. "I've found ways to survive and stay young through my magic, but I've never found true friends. I've never found happiness. I've had a hundred years alone."

"That's because the magic is evil," Alex said. "It's corrupting. You haven't made friends because the power makes you want to manipulate them."

"No. That's not true."

"We were nice to you and look how you're repaying it," Derek said.

"No. I won't listen to you."

He walked on over to the edge of the room and pulled back a cloth from small wax figures that stood on a makeshift altar only a couple of feet off the floor. There were four of them, each carefully molded into the shape of the monsters from the game.

Derek recognized Ogre, styled almost like a toy figure, each detail carefully realized. The same was true of each monster. Vapor was crafted as a rippled sheet of wax, much like a sculpture of waves in the parting of the Red Sea statue Derek had seen once. The others were crafted just as they had been described. The Feline was a replica of the creature they'd seen in the forest. Tyger was like a more ferocious version of some prehistoric saber-toothed tiger, larger with huge jaws.

Alex seemed to jump at the sight of his own monster. Derek found it somewhat unsettling to see Ogre as well. The demonic eyes and the hideous ridged skull seemed more frightening than he'd imagined.

"The figurines are necessary," Geoff explained. "Much as you might recognize a voodoo doll, these objects are used to make the monsters real. They give form to our imaginings."

"You'd have had only one if it weren't for us," Alex said.

"Yes. One person, one monster, you might say. It would be expecting too much of a single imagination to create more."

Turning his back to the group, Geoff took a folder of matches from his pocket and began to light candles, careful to place them far enough away from the monster figures to avoid melting them with the heat.

Chants began to rise from his lips, the odd-sounding words seeming to twist as they became audible. The effect was almost immediate. The figurines began to move then, as if they were awakening and stretching from a long slumber.

"I can't believe this is real," Paige whispered.

"It's like, like something from a special-effects movie."

"It's image magic," Alex said. "I read a little about it."

Derek twisted around. "It's our imagination that's fueling this. Is there some way we could, I don't know, refuse? Block it out?"

"Not at this point," Geoff said. He had turned from his small altar and was looking over his shoulder at them, smiling. "Didn't think I was listening? Too bad, you have no chance now. The monsters are formed."

The wax figures were beginning to grow, and sounds issued from them, sounds of stretching and pulsing as ripples spread through their limbs and bodies.

Geoff rose and opened the window, and as a wisp of night air swept in, the Feline figure moved, taking a couple of slow steps and then leaping gracefully to the windowsill. In a second it had disappeared through the opening. Tyger followed. Vapor had slowly changed from the solid statuette that represented her into an almost-transparent mist, and she rode the breeze outside.

Ogre seemed to be looking around for a moment. His slitted eyes had become real, and the intelligence Derek had imagined for him seemed to be reflected in his gaze. He was contemplating. Miming toward the kids, he gave a knowing nod, and then he quickly crawled through the opening before his expanding size made it impossible.

"They're off," Geoff said with a laugh, but he didn't sound funny. His eyes seemed to blaze. "Who knows what prizes they'll find? Tonight the game is real."

Derek closed his eyes, the thought of the monsters on the loose spinning horrible possibilities through his brain. They would rip Amber and Craig apart and devour their flesh. As mean as the snobs had been, he didn't wish that on them.

Slowly he opened his eyes again and let a smile spread across his face, a broad, friendly smile.

"You're making a good point," he said. "It's going to be wild."

Geoff looked at him cautiously. "You agree?"

"I've been watching you, thinking about what you said. There's a lot of people out there who deserve it. Those snobs will be sorry. If they get it, it'll be worth it, won't it?"

Geoff nodded and smiled, but he remained cautious. "I think you're seeing things from my perspective," he agreed. "Of course you could be bluffing."

"No, not a bluff at all," Derek said. "I've been thinking about what it must have been like for you. When you first saw the sorcerer work, I mean."

"It was exciting," Geoff said. "But it's hard to remember. It was a long time ago."

"Think about what you felt," Derek said. "That's what I'm feeling right now. I'm thinking of the possibilities of what I could learn from you."

"You creep," Paige said. "You're not thinking about joining up with this guy! You can't!"

"Don't try to play games," Geoff said. "You don't want to become a sorcerer."

117

"Sure I do," Derek said. "If it's anything like playing the Terror Club. I always got a real rush just from pretending to play with magical business. If I could learn the real thing, I could do whatever I wanted. I could get rid of Neil, my mom's boyfriend."

"You really dislike him that much?" Geoff asked.

"I don't think he's right for my mom, and more than anything that's what I want. To take care of him."

Geoff studied his face for a long time. "You have complained about him."

"He's a jerk. Can you show me how to get rid of him?"

"Derek, it's crazy. It's dangerous stuff," Paige pleaded.

"He's managed a hundred years at it," Derek said. "Show me, Geoff. Come on."

Slowly Geoff walked over to him, and kneeling, he reached back and loosened the bonds around Derek's wrists. That allowed Derek to pull his hands free.

"It's simple really," Geoff said. "I can show you some basic stuff right here."

His voice rose slightly, and he sounded like the Geoff they'd known all summer. His excitement and intensity were as strong as ever.

"A lot of it is in knowing the runic alphabet. You know about the runes in the packet. The tiles were pointless, a decoy item, but the runes were important."

Derek listened as he gave a brief explanation of the lettering system, and then he moved with Geoff over to the altar. "The monsters have been getting stronger each night as I've sent them forth. Tonight they're at their full strength."

"I can't believe you're going along with this," Alex said from across the room. "Sooner or later both of you are going to bite off something too big for you to handle."

"It's all a matter of being careful," Geoff said.

He turned to look at Alex, and as he did, Derek shoved his elbow into one of the candles. It toppled over, the flame touching the dried wood of the floor. The splinters quickly began to pop, and the fire licked almost hungrily across the boards.

"Oops," Derek said.

"What are you doing?" Geoff shouted, and quickly began yanking his jacket off to snuff out the flames. "You could start a forest fire if this place goes up."

As he swatted at the quickly spreading blaze, Derek scrambled across the room to Paige and Alex, freeing her first and then helping Alex get untied.

"You liar," Geoff shouted over his shoulder as he continued to fight the fire. He was having some success despite the fact that the whole building was kindling.

Ignoring his screams of anger, they headed for the exit.

Chapter Nineteen

Tyger

"**W**e've got to round up the monsters," Alex said as they hurried away from the house, letting the shadows conceal them.

After making their way through the cemetery, they found a spot under an oak tree for concealment.

"That was a pretty good acting job back there," Paige said. "You almost had me convinced, Derek."

"You did pretty good, too," Derek said. "I think calling me a creep helped convince him."

"Ms. Stone did her job," Alex said. "We just can't stop now. We've got one. A job, that is."

"Rounding up monsters is easier said than done," Derek observed. "We don't exactly have a way to control them."

"If they were created, at least partially by us, we should be able to destroy them," Alex speculated. "The runes he sent us were used to focus the energy of our imaginations. If we confront the monsters and then destroy the rune that represents each one, we might stand a chance."

"You've read this?"

"I'm speculating based on things I've read about how magic works or is supposed to work. I didn't think it was real until now. Is everybody carrying theirs?"

Derek patted his pocket.

"I've got mine," Paige said. "And Geoff's still got the Feline rune."

"We'll worry about that later," Alex said. "Since I was leading the game, Tyger hasn't been played that much. Even though he's bigger, he's probably not as powerful. Let's see if we can find him."

"Remember to watch out for Geoff," Paige said. "He's going to be after us soon."

"We'll have to take the rune away from him eventually," Alex said. "If he finds us, we'll overpower him—just watch out for the dagger."

"That's less to worry about than tiger claws," Paige said.

Cautiously, they made their way through the thick clusters of underbrush, looking for signs of the way the monsters had passed. There were some broken branches and some other marks of disturbance, but determining which creature had gone where was impossible.

"I guess we'll have to deal with them as we find them," Alex said.

"One monster at a time," Derek agreed, looking around. He could feel his fear building, and he knew if the others felt what he was feeling, absolute terror would not be long in coming.

Slowly, they looked around, then picked a direction arbitrarily and headed that way, clustered together. It was again like *The Wizard of Oz*.

When Derek noticed a fallen oak branch large enough to serve as a club, he grabbed it, breaking off stray twigs to make it usable. It wasn't the best weapon in the world, but it made sense to have something.

"Maybe I should find one, too," Alex said. For a few seconds they looked around until they located more sticks for Paige and Alex.

"At least we can swat at them a little," Alex said.

"They'll think they're getting mosquito bites," Paige observed.

Derek shrugged. "If they stop to scratch, at least we'll have a chance to run."

Turning their attention again to the matter of tracking, they advanced a little further through the woods. They were still spotting occasional signs of the monsters' movement, but they didn't really have a good idea of where they were headed.

"Is this how Tarzan would do it?" Derek asked. Alex stopped and snapped his fingers. "No, it's not, but it gives me an idea."

"That's better than we've done so far," Paige said. "What is it?"

"Tarzan climbs trees. If one of us climbed a tree, that could give a vantage," Alex said. "We might be able to get an idea of where the monsters are."

"Who's going to do the climbing?" Derek asked.

Both Paige and Alex looked at him.

"You're the most agile," Paige pointed out.

"That's not saying much," Derek said.

"Come on," Alex said. "I'll give you a leg up."

Derek couldn't argue. The idea made sense, so he helped with the selection of a tree, an oak with a slight slope to the trunk that would make scaling it a little easier.

Alex knelt, entwining his forgers into a stirrup, and Derek slipped his foot in. As Alex lifted, Derek clawed at the tree's bark, finding a few handholds, and with the slope and Paige pushing against his back, he managed to move upward to the first branches.

From there he was able to ascend quickly, working his way up the tree from branch to branch. He had a mild fear of heights, but he didn't look down.

As he moved higher, he began to gaze across the forest. He could see only other trees at first, but as he moved upward he began to see a little better. He could make out the trail they had traveled, and he could see other winding paths and rabbit runs.

"How is it?" Alex called from the ground.

"Nothing yet, but I have a pretty good view."

Much of the area was shrouded in shadow, but he could make out a great deal. As the bark scraped skin off his palms, he gritted his teeth. An ache was forming in his legs and lower back, but he knew he had to keep going.

Finally he reached a limb a number of feet off the ground. Lifting himself onto it and keeping near the tree trunk, he began to scan the forest floor.

Binoculars would've been handy, he thought, but he had to depend on his eyes.

Certainly things as large as the monsters would be visible, even in the darkness. He just had to spot them. Once while riding in a car, he had been surprised when he'd looked out the window and spotted a squirrel on the roadside. Its coat had allowed it to blend in with the background. Only its sudden movement gave it away, and the monsters had the same possibilities for invisibility. They would blend into the forest fairly well, especially with the darkness, but they couldn't remain totally concealed unless they were in hiding and still.

Squinting, he swept his gaze slowly from one side of the wood to the other. He was almost surprised when he managed to spot movement. Far over through a thicket, he could see Tyger crouched over something, the muscles in his striped back moving. Was he eating something? Maybe.

Derek made his way back down the tree as quickly as possible, trying to keep quiet. The other monsters might not be far away.

"What'd you see?" Alex asked when he touched down.

"Tyger, somewhere over this way. He was eating something."

"He'll really be mad if we bother him while he's having dinner," Paige said.

"He's not going to be happy to see us any time," Alex countered, picking up the sticks. "Let's go."

He tossed Derek a club, and they set off with Derek slightly in the lead. They had to travel through the thickest part of the forest, but without slowing down they batted vines and tangles out of their way with their makeshift weapons.

They were panting as they began to get near the spot where Derek had seen the creature. Sweat also soaked their clothes, so much it was almost as if they'd run through a row of lawn sprinklers.

"It's just ahead," Derek whispered, and they slowed their pace, creeping forward through a cluster of small bushes.

As they pushed the branches apart, they could see Tyger. He was on his stomach, gnawing on something.

"It's a rabbit," Alex whispered.

"The poor thing," Paige said.

"It'll be poor us if he turns around," Derek reminded.

"We have to confront him," Alex said. He reached into his pocket and pulled out the folded paper with the rune markings.

"Are we just going to walk up to him?" Derek asked.

"We created him, or I did. I ought to be able to un-create him."

"Where do you want me to send your things if that's wrong?" Derek asked.

Alex didn't laugh. He handed Derek his club and, grasping the rune with both hands, he moved forward.

"Wish me luck," he said.

The bushes rattled as he stepped through them. The sound made Tyger's ears twitch slightly, and his massive head turned.

Blood dripped from his jaws and covered the fur on his chin, and his eyes seemed to glow bright green as he looked back at Alex.

"He's going to eat him," Paige said.

"Maybe not," Derek whispered. He clutched the club tightly, ready to rush forward and pound the creature if necessary, whether or not it would do any good.

He watched Alex creep forward, and slowly, the monster turned and got to its feet. Standing, it was a massive beast, much larger than a regular tiger, almost as tall at the shoulder as a horse, and the teeth curved out of his mouth like knives.

"You were created from my imagination," Alex said. "It's time for you to go back there."

Tyger tilted his head slightly, as if trying to understand the words. After only a few seconds, he lowered his head, a deep, menacing growl forming somewhere inside him. The face was not the common face of a tiger at the zoo, Derek realized. There was an evil look about it, an ugliness he couldn't really define.

"You are not real," Alex said. "I imagined you."

The creature raised a paw and stepped forward, as if walking into range.

"Go away," Alex insisted. "Go away!"

He held the rune in the air over his head, stretching it out like a banner between his hands.

"I'm going to destroy the rune that made you possible."

Tyger hesitated, looking at the rune, eyes glowing brighter than ever.

"I think it's becoming transparent," Paige said.

Derek squinted and looked closely at the animal. "I think you're right," he agreed. It seemed he could see trees not just behind the creature but through him.

"I hope he disappears before he gets Alex," he said. "Can't we help?"

"I don't think so," Derek said. "It's his monster."

For a second, Tyger's tail twitched. The look of malevolence never left his features, and slowly his legs bent.

"He's crouching to jump," Paige said.

"Alex! He's about to—"

Before Derek could complete his sentence, the creature moved, muscles tensing, hind legs acting in a spring action.

The huge body was launched in the air, and the front claws extended. When he came down, the nails would dig into Alex and rip him apart even before the fangs could tear into his throat.

Derek started forward with the club raised, hoping he might block the onslaught.

Even as he moved, Alex was ripping the rune apart and protesting at the top of his lungs that Tyger was not real. The beast continued to angle forward, covering the short distance, drawing closer and closer to Alex's flesh.

Derek stopped in his tracks an instant before the claws would've made contact. Suddenly there was nothing there. Tyger had vanished, and only a swirl of tattered paper remained, twisting and floating about on the night breeze like a dust devil made of parchment fragments.

Alex sank to a seat on the ground, raising both hands to his face.

"You can't believe how glad I am that worked," he said.

"That's one down, and three to go," Paige said.

Alex swallowed, trying to regain composure. Even though he'd been successful, he was trembling. "I'm afraid the others won't be as easy to deal with as Tyger," he said.

Chapter Twenty

Knock Knock

Amber sat on her living-room sofa, tucked under her, and she leaned against the cushions for support as she dabbed at her nose with a tissue. Her eyes were swollen and red, and her hair was tangled. She looked like she'd been in a car wreck, Craig thought.

He was sitting at the opposite end of the sofa. She didn't want to be close to anyone right now. She was too upset by the deaths of her friends.

"We didn't even have one funeral yet," she said. "They're going to have to have them together, I guess."

"They won't do that," Craig said.

"They might," she said. "The parents are talking about it."

Her parents were visiting the Cradles tonight to offer their comfort even though formal visitation had not yet been scheduled by the funeral home. Craig had come over at their request so that Amber would not be alone.

He'd never felt more inadequate. He never knew how to handle it when Amber was in a bad mood, and this was worse than ever.

He didn't know what to say or what to do, and she wasn't giving any clues about what might make her feel better.

"You want something to drink?" he asked.

Her answer was only a nod. He got up and headed into the kitchen. Swinging open the refrigerator, he found a couple of soft drinks tucked into slots on the door.

He selected a Coke for her and a Dr. Pepper for himself. His mother had always ordered him to wrap napkins around drinks when serving them, but he didn't feel like bothering. Amber wasn't going to notice.

He was headed back to the couch when he heard the knock at the front door. It wasn't exactly a knock, however. It was more like a thud, as if something hard and solid had struck the door.

He walked across the living room, planning to look out through the narrow window beside the door. He never got the chance. A second later, the door crashed inward, the facing splintering, and the hinges ripping free.

He had no time to run, no time to do anything. He stood frozen, looking out into the darkness. Something moved, something big.

Amber screamed.

Craig did, too.

Chapter Twenty-One

Vapor

"Which one do we go after next?" Paige asked.

"It doesn't matter," Alex said. He was rubbing his neck now, trying to get calm. "They're probably all equally as strong."

"So it's whichever one we come across?" Paige asked.

"Or whichever one runs across us first," Derek said. "If it's the Feline, we have a problem."

"Let's roll," Alex said. He picked up his club again, and he and Derek walked shoulder to shoulder with Paige close behind.

Sticking to the trail, they stepped only a few paces at a time, pausing to look about through the trees and brush for indications of the monsters.

With each breath, Derek expected something to pounce from the darkness, something that would rip them apart or crush them.

The job seemed too big, too frightening, a task that should not have been thrust upon people so young, but who else was there? This was their fight, to the finish.

At a point Derek estimated as the forest's center, they spotted a footprint, another deep mark from Ogre's foot.

"He could be somewhere in the shadows," Alex said.

Derek looked around. He had sensed Ogre's actions before, but that connection seemed to be gone now. The creature was on his own and could strike without warning and destroy before the rune could be ripped apart. That didn't sound like fun.

"I wish we had a flashlight or something," Alex said.

"There was no way to plan for that," Paige said. "Our bad luck," Alex observed. "We'll have to keep feeling our way along."

"Until we bump into something furry," Derek said. He reached out and squeezed Paige's hand. Too bad they hadn't met under other circumstances. They could've had a great summer.

Now it would be nice if they just managed to stay alive.

Listening, Derek tried to pick out some sound that might point them in the direction of a monster. Crickets chirped, branches rattled in the breeze and other night sounds accompanied them, but he couldn't detect anything like the rasp of breath or heavy footfalls.

He grabbed Alex's arm. "They must know we're looking for them," he said.

"Maybe they figured it out after we got Tyger."

"Could be. They must be waiting for us to come to them."

"They figure that's easier," Alex said. "They can anticipate our moves because we've been playing them for weeks. They understand our strategy and thinking."

"The whole game was based on stalking," Paige said.

Derek snapped his fingers. "Yeah, maybe we should make them come to us."

Alex dropped to one knee. "Worth a try. Be ready to confront whoever shows up."

Waiting was worse than hunting. As they sat back to back, keeping watch in all directions, the seconds seemed to be riding on the backs of turtles. Nothing happened for what seemed an eon.

Derek could feel his stomach churning now, the fear threatening to make him hurl. If he'd eaten more recently, he might've. His mom must've come home by now. Alex's parents were worried. Paige's were probably frantic. How long would it take someone to find them? By now someone should be looking. They'd called cops the last time!

It didn't make sense. Not unless the families had already checked the forest and failed to find any sign of the kids. How could they miss the car, though? It would be parked at the edge of the wood, and that would be a clear sign the kids were in here.

Unless …

"I think I know where Vapor is," he said.

Paige tugged her rune from her pocket. "Where?"

"At the front of the wood," Derek said. "Providing cover."

"How do you know?" Alex asked.

"That's why nobody's been able to find us. Vapor's got the front of the wood covered, looking like a fog and hiding anything she doesn't want people to see. If anyone passed looking for us, they'd never see my car out there, and if they tried to look it would be impossible."

"You're right," Alex said. "She could fool them easily."

"I guess we know which one we deal with now," Paige said. "Remember, she'll be able to bounce emotions back at us."

They set off as quickly as the tangled trail would allow. They managed to maintain a light trot, jumping over things that were in their way.

As they neared the front of the forest, the smoke-like shroud became visible in the moonlight. It was like a thick dose of the usual mists that form in a forest at night, but there was no doubting the origin.

"I guess this one is mine," Paige said, drawing a deep breath to prepare herself. She shivered in spite of the heat.

With Derek and Alex behind her to fend off any other creatures that might arrive, she began to approach Vapor much as Alex had done his monster.

The mist reacted almost immediately, twisting slightly, then swirling. Vapor had been stretched into a broad blanket, but now she drew into a more concentrated cloud, like the spew from a genie's bottle.

She had no true shape, no real form, but she was there, ready, dangerous.

"Go away, Vapor!"

Paige's rebuke was almost a shriek. She stopped walking about ten feet in front of the cloud which towered over her in a vertical pattern. From where Derek stood it looked as if she were confronting a massive polar bear.

As he tried to remain calm, he felt his fear intensifying, Vapor's power at work.

"I don't believe in you," Paige said. "I imagined you. Now I'm dismissing you."

Vapor began to twist about more, and for a moment it seemed she was about to dissipate. He thought she was going to disappear just the way Tyger had, but the cloud had surprises yet to offer.

Instead of disappearing, Vapor only stretched herself out a little, forming a wide cloud as thick as smoke.

Paige screamed another rebuke, but almost before the last word had tumbled from her lips, Vapor swirled around her, enveloping her.

"It's got her!" Derek screamed. He started to rush forward to pull her out, but Alex grabbed his arm. "It'll only swallow you, too," he said.

"No," Derek shouted. Tears came to his eyes as he watched Vapor's pulsing form, expanding and contracting as if she was digesting.

"We've got to help her," he said.

"I don't know what to do," Alex shouted. Helplessly, Derek continued to stare forward, wishing there were some kind of answer.

"We can fan it," he said. "Ogre tried different things that worked in the game. Remember? That might work in reality."

"That might," Alex agreed.

They quickly broke leaf-covered branches from the nearby bushes and began to wave them frantically toward the cloud. The motion generated a quick breeze that pushed at the edge of the haze but didn't disperse it.

"Move closer," Derek shouted, and they inched forward, continuing to wave the fronds frantically.

Through the mist, he could make out Paige's form. She was still standing upright, but he wasn't sure if she was alive or being supported somehow by the cloud.

"Wave harder," he cried. The fear was almost unbearable, but he couldn't turn back. Paige couldn't be dead, not because of some stupid game. He loved her.

"Paige!" he shouted, but no sound escaped the mass.

Frantically, Derek waved harder, creating an even-stronger breeze, and Alex pumped his arms harder also, fanning as if he were trying to turn back a hurricane.

Inside the cloud, Paige seemed to be jostling about. That could mean Vapor was devouring her. Derek wanted to dive forward and yank her out, but he knew that might only wind up getting them both suffocated.

If they could get her out, there might still be time for first aid. He'd studied mouth-to-mouth resuscitation in a health class last year.

Fanning even harder, he watched the cloud begin to dissipate.

131

"It's getting there," Alex said.

"Keep it up," Derek called. He felt the muscles in his arms beginning to ache, but he knew he couldn't relent.

The breeze pushed deeper into the cloud now, changing the shape, pushing it about. Slowly at first and then more quickly the cloud began to fragment and spread away from the wind gusts.

"It's going," Alex said.

They forced themselves to keep waving. Slowly at first and then almost immediately the cloud parted, dissolving. As it disappeared, Paige slumped to the ground.

Derek ran to her, kneeling at her side and sliding his arms around her.

"Paige, please be all right," he shouted.

Her eyes fluttered open, and her lungs expelled air in a quick, relieved gasp.

He realized her hands were filled with the tattered remains of the rune, and as she opened her fingers, the scraps seemed almost magically to float from her palms onto the wind.

"I can hold my breath a long time," she reminded.

"I forgot about our swimming trip. I thought it was chewing you up, but you were tearing up the rune."

"I had to keep fighting," she said.

"It worked."

They hugged each other until Alex stepped over. "Come on," he said. "The Feline and Ogre are still around somewhere."

He handed Derek his club, and they turned back toward the Nightmare Wood. The shadows did not give any indication of where the other monsters might be hiding.

"Where do you suppose they are?" Paige asked. "Right up here," came a voice.

They looked upward into an oak tree with long, twisted branches. Geoff and the Feline were side by side in the nook of a thick branch.

The sorcerer had his knife drawn, and the Feline was crouched with claws extended.

Chapter Twenty-Two

Geoff and The Feline

"You might have been able to get rid of the others, but I've got the rune for this one," Geoff chided.

The Feline's head tilted, and its mouth opened in a sudden, piercing shriek, revealing again the long, sharp teeth.

"Ready to be ripped to shreds?" Geoff asked. "Not yet," Derek responded.

"Too bad."

Geoff patted the cat-creature's shoulder, prompting the monster to make its lunge.

As it plunged downward, Alex drew his club back as if it were a Louisville slugger and swung hard as the creature came into range. The blow caught the Feline on the side of its head just below one of the long pointed ears.

Despite its graceful moves, the sudden hit confused it, and it landed on the ground with an awkward thud.

"It's not quite like a real cat," Paige said.

"We're not quite like Meow Mix either, but the difference doesn't matter in the big picture," Alex said, pushing them deeper into the forest as the Feline began to reorient itself.

"You'll never get away," Geoff taunted.

They ducked under some vines and moved down a slope made rugged from drainage, leaping across a narrow ditch at the bottom.

The crevice was not that deep, but it was hard to see in the darkness and could've caused injury if they had stepped into it.

Alex and Derek seemed to have the realization at the same time, and, turning to each other, they nodded.

"We should cover it," Paige said, obviously on the same wavelength.

"Like an elephant pit," Alex said.

Scrambling about, they snatched up pieces of wood and debris, vines, brush, and leaves and used them to conceal the indentation.

"Keep moving now," Alex said.

They turned and hurried up the opposite rise, which sloped upward only a short distance before leveling off. Bushes lined the top edge of the grade, so they concealed themselves there.

"He shouldn't be that far behind us," Paige said. "Not far," Alex agreed. "Just give him a few seconds."

As if in answer to his suggestion, the Feline appeared at the top of the opposite slope. Pausing there, the creature reared on its hind legs, sniffing the air. Even at the distance they could detect the twitching of his large nose and whiskers.

He seemed to get an answer from the air, and quickly, he began to move down the rough ground on all fours again.

Derek watched the descent in the light that filtered down through the trees. The monster stepped with sure-footed ease.

About halfway down, he paused, sniffing the air again. Derek held his breath. Something was wrong. The creature was suspicious. Instead of rushing downward quickly in an effort to catch up with them, it was being cautious.

"It's not going to work," Paige said.

"It would've been too easy," Alex said. "We got rid of the others without a hitch. Our luck was bound to run out. We don't have the rune, and he's about to figure out our trap."

And he did.

At the edge of the ditch, the Feline sniffed, then pawed at the sticks and other cover and discovered the space beneath.

After raking the conglomeration aside so that it no longer covered the ditch, he hopped across and started to move upward. At the same moment, Geoff came bounding down the opposite side to catch up with his monster.

"Time to go," Alex said.

He got no arguments. Paige and Alex followed him back through the trees. They were in a part of the forest they had never fully explored, but Derek sensed they were moving away from the roadway.

He'd practically abandoned hope anyway that anyone might show up to help. Vapor's protecting shroud was gone, but even if people tried to locate them now they'd be so far out of sight it might not matter. "We're going to have to find a way to get that rune again," he said as they jogged along.

"It's going to be hard to make him fall for any more tricks," Paige said. "Even with our acting lessons."

"We could come up with something he might believe," Alex said.

"Like what?"

Derek stopped them. "What if he thinks we ditched Paige?"

"You mean me convince him you guys left me?"

"It might work. It would at least get him close," Derek said.

"We're just going to be dodging the Feline until he wears us out and eats us," she said. "It's worth a try. You guys will stay close, though?"

"Yeah," Alex said. "Very close."

"So all we've got to do is find him."

"Or let him find us."

Brushing back some leaves on the forest floor, they found some dirt, which was applied to Paige's face to make it more believable that she'd fallen down. Then they selected a spot under a tree for her to sit.

"What if the Feline eats me first?" she asked.

"We'll jump him before that happens," Alex said.

Leaving her, they ducked back in underbrush. They would still have the Feline's sense of smell to contend with, but this seemed to be the best chance they had.

They didn't have to wait long for Geoff to catch up. He was moving along at the monster's side, letting it lead him through the shadows.

"Help," Paige called as he moved into view.

He stopped, placing a hand on the creature's side to slow it as well. It seemed obedient to him even though it towered over him.

"What is it?"

"Please don't hurt me," Paige whimpered. She wiped her eyes as if she were fighting tears. "They left me."

135

Geoff walked forward. "I'm supposed to believe your boyfriend and buddy left you?"

"I couldn't keep up, and they were scared. They said they had to save themselves."

"How do I know this isn't another trick?"

She sobbed.

Listening from his hiding place, Derek had to admit she was convincing, employing the acting skills well. He curled his fingers tightly around his club, ready to use it if anything went wrong. The sweat along his spine had grown cold, and he shuddered as the night breeze swept around him. Waiting was the worst, he repeated to himself

"Derek just left you?" Geoff was asking. He didn't believe her.

"Yes. I never would've thought he would do that."

"Neither would I."

The Feline paused, standing just behind him, and its whiskers began to twitch.

The movement caught Geoff's eye, and he looked up at the creature. Then he realized what it was smelling, and he turned, looking toward the brush where the other boys were hiding.

He was going to shout, to order the Feline to attack, but as he raised his hand to point, Paige shot forward from her spot at the base of the tree.

Wrapping her arms around his legs and shoving herself forward, she threw him off balance. He flailed his arms in an effort to remain standing, but he couldn't stay on his feet.

He fell back against the Feline, thudding into its furry side and taking it by surprise. The cat-thing let out a sudden screech as it staggered backward.

Derek and Alex left their hiding places then and charged. Alex raised his club again, heading for the Feline, while Derek joined Paige in the struggle with Geoff.

Though Geoff wasn't a large person, he twisted and squirmed, violently swinging his arms and fists. He slammed one blow into Derek's collar bone, and the pain spread through the shoulder instantly.

"Get the rune!" Alex shouted, just managing to dodge a swipe from the Feline's massive front paw.

"We're trying," Paige said. She could feel the folded paper in the pocket of Geoff's shirt, but he was making every effort to keep her from tugging it free.

Derek climbed on top of him as he tried to slap Paige.

"No!" Geoff shouted. "I won't let you. I won't let you!"

Grabbing his wrists, Derek pushed his arms to the ground and held them so Paige could pull the note free.

"Let's go," Alex screamed again, and he made the mistake of looking back to check their progress.

The Feline managed to swipe its paw past the stick Alex had been using to bat its claws away, and the sharp nails slashed across his face and neck, digging deep cuts through his flesh.

He was knocked to the ground, stunned and bleeding.

As the cat started to raise another claw, Derek hurled himself off Geoff's chest and picked up the club he'd dropped. He gripped it tightly and slammed it against the creature's head, trying to aim for the same spot Alex had clipped it before. He reasoned that spot would be a tender one.

The cat eyes flared angrily as the pain rattled it. With mouth open it turned on Derek. Now he knew how Tweety Bird felt.

Geoff wanted to laugh, but Paige shoved her knee down onto his hand and managed at last to grab the rune.

"We've got you," she said. She ripped the paper apart before he could stop her.

"You can't destroy my monster," he cried.

No one listened as the Feline's form began to flicker. For a moment, Geoff's unwillingness to release it from his imagination kept it standing, but as Derek and Paige willed it to disappear, it slowly began to become transparent.

The creature seemed confused for a moment, as if it had just awakened from sleep.

"I won't will him away," Geoff protested. "I won't."

Derek closed his eyes and concentrated. They had to overpower Geoff's will. He forced himself not to think of the Feline, to imagine it was not there.

Gradually the creature began to flicker even more. The combined wills were too strong, and he disappeared into nothingness.

"You killed him," Geoff said. "Killed him."

"He almost killed Alex," Derek responded, kneeling at his friend's side.

"I'm not dead," Alex said, misunderstanding the others.

"I know," Derek said. "We'll get you help as soon as possible."

"But Ogre's still out there," Paige said.

"Yeah," Geoff said. "Your own monster. The smart monster. You'll never outwit him. He's been waiting for you all night."

"He'll never let us out of the forest alive," Alex said. "You've got to get him."

"But what about you?"

"I'll be okay."

"You have to stay with him," Derek told Paige after they'd tied Geoff to a tree.

"You're going after Ogre alone?"

"I made him. I started it all. I gave Geoff the way to work his magic. I have it to do."

"Be careful," she whispered.

He kissed her softly. "I'll be fine."

He wished he could believe his own reassurance.

Chapter Twenty-Three

Ogre

Derek patted his pocket to make sure the rune was there. He didn't want to be caught without it, not when he found Ogre. Or Ogre found him.

As he leaned against the base of a tree, trying to catch his breath, he realized how frightened he had become. A knot of fear as cold as a serpent had coiled inside him. And he'd thought this summer was going to be boring.

One lousy ad had changed all that. One ad and a sorcerer, he corrected himself. The magazine wasn't responsible for Geoff.

Derek felt responsible, however. He hoped Alex was going to be all right. He had to stop Ogre before anyone else got hurt, even the snobs.

He tried to think of how Ogre had functioned in the games. He had frequently outwitted his opponents. He had been cautious most of all. That explained why he was still at large.

He wasn't hiding, but he was somewhere safe, somewhere they wouldn't be likely to look. He was there waiting, Derek knew.

Ogre would realize they would come for him, and he would realize Derek would find him. That would be inevitable since they thought alike.

That's what Ogre wanted. The monster would try to destroy Derek before Derek could destroy the rune.

He patted his pocket again. What if he tore the rune up here, without confronting Ogre? Would that work? He knew, somewhere deep inside, that it would not. He'd have to be face-to-face with the monster's hideous countenance. He'd have to look into those horrible eyes.

Only then would it be banished.

Unmaking monsters was much more frightening than making them.

Closing his eyes, he concentrated on getting his fear under control. He couldn't think in a state of terror. He took several long, slow breaths.

As he began to relax, he let his imagination flow. Where would Ogre go?

He jerked forward from the tree a few seconds later. He knew where Ogre was. He knew why he hadn't run across him as they had crisscrossed the forest. He wasn't in the Nightmare Wood.

Ogre would be back at the caretaker's house. The creature knew they would be busy looking for monsters in the woods, so that was the safest place around.

Picking up his stick, Derek headed that way.

The front door was partially open. Through the crack, he could see only darkness inside. He paused at the edge of a row of headstones. He didn't really want to go in, but he didn't have much of a choice. Slowly, he walked forward, listening for some sound of Ogre as he edged forward, but he couldn't even make out the rasp of the creature's breathing.

Maybe he wasn't in there.

Only one way to find out.

He cautiously placed his foot on the first step. Ogre would know he was coming, but he didn't want to announce his approach with creaking boards.

He placed his feet down softly as he moved up onto the porch. He was holding the stick in both hands, his arms slightly cocked and ready to strike if necessary. The stick wouldn't do much good against Ogre. Still, he hoped it would at least keep him busy.

With his left foot, Derek shoved the door open, then stepped across the threshold. He expected to see Ogre standing, waiting for him, but at first glance the room appeared to be empty.

"Who's that?" someone said in a quavering voice.

As his eyes slowly adjusted to the darkness, Derek realized two people were sitting on the floor against the wall. Craig and Amber huddled together. All of their previous signs of condescension and arrogance were gone. They were victims now

"Derek? Is that you?" Craig asked.

"It's me," Derek whispered. He rushed over, freeing them from the bonds that held their wrists and feet.

"This … th-this thing came and got us," Amber said.

"I know," Derek said.

"Is it from that stupid game of yours?"

"It's from Geoff. He's trying to kill everybody."

"Let's get out of here."

"No snide remarks for me?"

"Sorry about all that," Craig said.

"Where'd the monster go?"

"I think he left."

Cautiously, Derek looked around. Only a pile of ashes and charred wood remained where Geoff had stomped out the fire.

The only spot he hadn't checked was…

The corner behind the door!

He heard the door hinge squeak and started to turn—wasn't fast enough.

The strong, furry paw closed around his collar and he was lifted from the floor. He kicked and flailed, unable to make contact as he dangled, held by his own shirt.

He twisted slightly, but he was still facing away from the monster. Hot breath tickled at the back of his neck, making the hairs stand up.

"Hello, Derek."

The voice was a rattle, deep and hoarse, spoken by lips not accustomed to forming words.

"You can talk?"

"I'm learning."

Ogre had been the first creature dreamed up. He was hyperintelligent. It made sense that he'd managed to learn language.

"You want to kill me."

"Not kill you. You're not real."

"I'm real. I won't let you destroy me."

Fingers quickly crawled across Derek's shirt, locating the folded square of paper easily. Derek grabbed at the thick, hairy wrist, but he wasn't strong enough to hold it. He felt the rune slide from his pocket, and his hope of surviving seemed to spill out of him as he was shoved back into the others.

There would be no stopping the creature now. He had hostages, and he had confiscated the only means of destroying him. Ogre would have free run of the town. With Derek out of the way, it might be impossible to get rid of him. He would rescue Geoff, and they would try to finish Geoff 's crazed plan.

He couldn't let Ogre do that. He had to find a way. He ran at the monster and began to kick at him, trying to do some damage. Amber and Craig remained pressed against the back wall.

Derek's attack seemed only to anger Ogre, who tossed him across the room with an easy flip of his arm.

Crashing into the wall with a thud, Derek sank to the floor. He lay still for a moment, letting the waves of pain in his head settle down. Then he rolled over and looked across the room. He could see a portion of Ogre's form outlined in the doorway, one massive arm, one tree trunk of a leg, the formidable slope of a shoulder.

"You cannot stop me."

"You're from my imagination."

"Not completely. Ogre is born of sorcery."

"Give me the paper," Derek demanded. With an effort he pushed himself into a sitting position on the floor. The crash had blurred his vision, and his head felt funny, but he wasn't going to give up. He'd jump on Ogre and grab for the paper if he had to.

"You will not destroy Ogre."

"You shouldn't be real, Ogre. You're part of a game."

He saw movement. Ogre was shaking his head, and his coarse breath rasped several times in succession. He was laughing.

Then, slowly, he turned and walked toward Craig and Amber. Deep in his throat a guttural growl rumbled.

Derek was stunned, but he pushed himself up and spun around. Ogre was going to kill them. In a flash, Derek realized the monster had not brought them as hostages. He would want to make it look like Derek was responsible.

The authorities would think Derek had gone nuts playing the game, and even if his friends backed him up they'd be dismissed as suffering from the same psychosis.

It was brilliant on Ogre's part. Derek would be locked up, and people would not even believe a huge hairy beast was at large.

The creature advanced, ready to slam a blow into the couple, probably one strong enough to take off a head.

"No!" Derek shouted. As much as he'd disliked the two, he didn't want them getting killed, and he didn't want to be blamed. He'd never intended Ogre to do evil, but Ogre was his monster.

The command made Ogre hesitate, and Craig and Amber inched away from him, though only slightly.

"Where'd it come from?" Amber whimpered.

"Ancient magic," Derek said. He slid his hand along the floor. His stick had rolled across the room, out of reach, but if he could find something else, anything, maybe a loose board. Then with Craig's help he could take care of the creature.

"Ogre will not let you hurt him."

"Why can it talk?" Amber asked.

"It's intelligent," Derek said.

"Ogre will kill you!"

The monster turned again toward the snobs.

At almost the same instant, Derek's fingers slipped over something, not a brick or board, something much smaller.

Matches.

Matches!

Geoff's matches, used for lighting the candles. They must have been kicked across the room in the scramble to put out the fire.

Now they might come in handy.

Ogre was advancing slowly, backing the kids into a corner. He was going to kill slowly too.

Derek got to his feet. A swell of dizziness swept up through him as he tried to stand. He'd hit the wall harder than he'd realized. He thought for a moment he was going to faint, but he had to move, had to get to the monster.

Tearing a match from the book, he fumbled with the packet. For a second he couldn't find the striking surface, but then his fingertip discovered the rough strip.

Staggering as quickly as he could across the room, he struck the match, and as it blazed bright orange, he touched the flame to Ogre's fur.

The matted coat ignited in an instant, and the dry hair became a blanket of flame. Suddenly the darkness from the room was gone. It was filled with an almost-blinding light.

A scream of anguish, of agony, issued from the monster's mouth, and it turned away from the two. Still clutching the rune in one hand, Ogre tried to reach to his back with the other. Frantically he sought to swat out the fire, but he could do little to extinguish himself.

Derek was stunned, frozen in place as the monster screamed again and twisted about at the center of the room. Craig bolted quickly from the corner, leading Amber with a sheltering arm toward the doorway.

Derek allowed him to lead the way away from the flame as it continued to consume Ogre. In a moment, the fire would find the rune, and he would be gone, just like the others. He willed the monster to disappear.

Still watching the fire, he backed through the door-way. He needed to get to safety in case Ogre caught the house on fire. As he stepped onto the porch, Geoff was there, still clutching his knife.

"You ruined everything," he said.

Derek turned to look at him.

His face was dirty, and blood from a scratch on his cheek had smeared down the side of his face. He might have looked pitiful if not for the madness in his eyes.

"You killed all my monsters."

Another scream issued through the door, a bellow from Ogre's massive lungs.

Derek could hear his footsteps behind him, thudding across the plank floor. He knew the monster was going to try to run out of the building even though he was ablaze.

Being caught between a flaming monster and a knife-wielding sorcerer didn't leave many options. "We're going to help Ogre," Geoff said.

"He'll be gone in a second. It'll be over. He was holding the rune."

"No, we can save him."

Derek pretended that he would turn as if preparing to go back in the cabin, but instead, he dove to one side, getting out of the doorway and rolling across the porch.

An instant later, Ogre broke through. He wasn't furry anymore. He was a walking mass of flame, and he slammed into Geoff before the sorcerer knew what was happening. They went tumbling in a tangled mass onto the porch floor, and Geoff screamed as the flames licked over him.

Derek tried to rush forward to pull him out, but the fire was too hot, hotter than it should have been, hotter than hell itself. He jumped from the porch as the fire mushroomed into a billowing orange cloud, a flare that seemed to light up the night.

That lasted only for an instant.

A second later, the fire was gone, and nothing … nothing at all remained.

Epilogue

A Lazy Summer Afternoon

A week later, Derek still had a knot on his head, but he was feeling better when Paige came to visit. She looked more beautiful than ever in a yellow pullover and black shorts with streaks of magenta and bright green in the pattern.

His mom, who had taken some time off from work to be with him, allowed them to walk outside to get some sunshine and talk in private even though she'd been watching him closely the last few days.

"I just visited Alex, too," Paige said. "He's doing a lot better. His dad got him a new Tolkien art book to look over while he recuperates, so he's happy. He wants you to come see him when you can."

"They're not letting me drive yet. Maybe Neil can give me a lift over."

"So you're talking to Neil, now, eh?"

"He's an okay guy. I guess I should've given him a chance earlier."

"I was glad he showed up looking for you the other night. I never would've gotten Alex out of the forest alone. I'm sorry Geoff got away and came after you."

"I managed. Hey, Craig and Amber didn't hesitate to hightail it."

"No, but I think they have a little more respect for you now."

"That makes me feel much, much better. I suspect their folks will have them seeing high-priced therapists for a while."

They walked along the driveway. Derek thought about holding her hand, but he figured his mom would be watching from the living-room window.

"Maybe we can go to the movies or something in a couple of days."

"I'd like that. I like spending time with you, but no more Terror Club games," she said.

"You don't have to worry about that," Derek said with a laugh. "I'm through with terror."

As they laughed, the white mail van pulled to a stop in front of the house, and the postman quickly tucked the day's mail into the box.

Watching the van speed away, Derek and Paige walked on to the box.

A large white envelope with red-and-blue stripes around the edges was inside, addressed to Derek. When he ripped it open, he was surprised to find several pieces of paper.

On top was a colorful drawing. It depicted a large, hairy beast with a ridged skull and wide catlike eyes. The second piece of paper was a letter:

> *Congratulations, Derek:*
>
> *We're sorry it's taken so long, but we're happy to announce you're a winner. Your monster has been chosen to appear in an upcoming issue of Scare. You'll find the artist's rendering of your creature enclosed. That's how he'll appear in our pages. Now you can also pit your monster against others by mail when you play—THE TERROR CLUB...*

About the Author

Sidney Williams is the author of numerous novels including the Si Reardon thrillers, *Fool's Run* and *Long Waltz*. His books from Crossroad Press include the slasher thriller *Dark Hours* and the Lovecraftian action-adventure novel *Disciples of the Serpent*. Sidney's short stories have appeared in numerous publications including *Cat Ladies of the Apocalypse*, *Love Among the Thorns*, *Deranged* and the upcoming *Unknown Heroes vs. the Forces of Darkness*. Sidney's first novels were released by Pinnacle Books. Those include *Blood Hunter*, *When Darkness Falls* and the possession thriller *Azarius*. He wrote several YA books under the name Michael August.

A former newspaper reporter, Sidney is now an adjunct professor of creative writing. He is originally from Louisiana and spent several years in Orlando. He now resides in Virginia with his wife and their cat Zoë Moonshadow.

Visit him at SidIsAlive.com, Facebook.com/SidneyWilliamsBooks for occasional flash fiction or seek him out as Willysid on TikTok for microfiction.

Sign up for his newsletter at sidneyw.substack.com.

Curious about other Crossroad Press books? Stop by our website:
http://crossroadpress.com
We offer quality writing
in digital, audio, and print formats.

Subscribe to our newsletter on the website homepage and receive a free
eBook.